TAMING THE TIGER

A F.U.C. ACADEMY STORY

SCARLET FOX

Produced in Canada

An EveL Worlds Production : www.worlds.EveLanglais.com

ACKNOWLEDGMENTS

I would like to thank Eve for letting me write in her world.

I would also like to thank Jessica for suggesting that I write in Eve's world and for all her help with the edits. "Light and fluffy" doesn't come easy to me, and Jessica really helped me with that vibe and to make this story really shine.

Thank you to Devin for the amazing edits and encouraging comments!

I also want to thank Rebecca Poole for the amazing cover art. The characters are exactly as I imagined them!

And a big thank you to every reader, for giving this book a chance!

~Scarlet

1

Paige Brennon ran until her throat burned, her chest tightened, and she thought for sure that her lungs would collapse.

And then she ran some more.

She weaved through the brown cornstalks—determined to prove you couldn't catch *this* tiger by the tail—until a pile of rocks in the center of the cornfield tripped her up, causing her body to spill into the moist dirt. *Just what I needed, a mud bath,* she thought with a grimace. She'd been on the move for what felt like hours, and the cool mud soothed her sore muscles, but Paige had to keep going. Though she needed a break, she couldn't afford to chance it if she was, indeed, being followed.

The escape was too easy, she thought for the millionth time. There was no reason for the door to her room to have been left unlocked, nor any reason for the tie on her right wrist to be *just* loose enough to wiggle out of. The people experimenting on her may have been asshats, but they weren't *stupid* asshats. Which meant it had to be a trap.

The scientists want to know what their little experiment is capable of, so they let *me escape.* They had to be tailing her, waiting to find out what she could do with her new abilities.

Whatever the hell they were.

A loon wailed in the distance, causing the hair on the back of her neck to rise at the sound. *I have to get out of here!*

Digging her nails into the muck—a reminder of the recent rain—she pulled herself to her feet, despite how much her aching muscles protested and threatened to seize. Paige ignored them as she pressed her bare feet into the cool earth, allowing it to squish between her toes.

She could have crossed more distance in her tiger form, but unfortunately, the jerks back at the laboratory had taken precautions to ensure that wasn't an option. The constant drip of some sort of sedative concoction into her veins had left a cool, tingling sensation throughout her blood vessels—while also taking away her shifting ability. Though it had been hours since she'd ripped the IV out, the effects still lingered.

The thought of shifting brought a fuzzy memory forward. Though she couldn't remember much from her life before the lab, she could at least recall that, as a child, she and her father would shift into their Siberian tiger forms and run through the forest, the tall Canadian pines creating the perfect jungle. What pained her most was having the memory, yet not being able to recall his name or the details of his face. It was as if his features were blurred out, his name forgotten, the complete image of him unable to be pieced together by her mind. But Paige could recall his fur in his tiger form, his scent, and the softness of his coat. All the other details slid through her fingers like grains of sand through a sieve.

But that was when the memories started to blur. Paige couldn't remember a thing past high school. She would bet her tail that the lab had done something to cloud her mind.

Paige wasn't even sure where they'd taken her. *Am I still in Canada?* She knew that she grew up near Barrie, Ontario. What she didn't know was her age—or even her location of residence—when she'd been captured. Vague memories of her childhood were the ones with the most detail. After what Paige had just been through, she felt old and worn out, but she knew that she couldn't have been more than thirty. She hoped accurate knowledge about herself would come with time, as she yearned to gain a better understanding of who she was and who she could become once she healed from the trauma—if she could get safely away.

Right now, all that mattered was her newfound

freedom. What she wouldn't give for some chocolate. It had been so long since she had some she could hardly remember the richness of it on her tongue. How it soothed her soul after having a bad day. And these last few months were a never-ending bad day. And though the sweet candy couldn't solve her problems, she knew it would still make her feel a hell of a lot better. Paige could practically feel it melting in her mouth.

It all abruptly slipped from her fingers when she reached the edge of the field, rounding a corner just to spot a man wearing a white lab coat, writing furiously on the clipboard he held.

Paige slowed to a walk as she approached him, and he looked up from his notes while the setting sun basked his angular features in an orange glow. "Excellent speed," he said as if she'd just completed a test that she'd had any knowledge of. "Though we'd hoped you would shift. We should have decreased the chemical inhibitor sooner." His cold voice sent a shiver down Paige's spine. It was Dr. Green. He took a step forward, raising what appeared to be a taser in his right hand. His black eyes seemed to absorb the light of the sun.

Paige glared at him as the heat rose in her cheeks. *The nerve of this guy, talking like I asked for this.* His audacity boiled her blood.

Dr. Green chuckled as a wicked smile spread across his aged face, illuminating his every wrinkle. "I see you're angry. No worries, that's what this is for," he said, nodding toward the taser. "No matter how strong we make you, we'll always have something stronger on hand to take you down."

Before he could use the device, the fury bubbled out of Paige, erupting as an ear-piercing scream, catching both her and the scientist off-guard. He dropped the clipboard and taser onto the grass as he slapped his hands to his ears, but it was too late for him—blood already trickled down either side of his neck.

That's new, she thought as she seized the opportunity to double back, returning to the cornfield and leaving Dr. Green behind.

Jake Park sat in his oversized FUC-issued SUV across the street from what appeared to be an abandoned warehouse. FUC—the Furry United Coalition, a protection agency that did whatever was needed to keep shifters safe and humans in the dark—had identified the building as a suspected illegal lab. One of many that had popped up in recent years to experiment on shifters and humans alike—turning humans into shifters and shifters into more powerful hybrid shifters.

The business was bad news for everyone involved.

Jake shifted in his seat. He was on his fourth hour of surveillance, and his back was killing him. *So glad they sent me here to watch nothing happen, aside from the few newspaper tumbleweeds blowing by.* He'd started to doubt that the intel was good. Not only were there so many illegal labs out there, but the criminals had started setting up decoy facilities to throw FUC off, so it was becoming more and more difficult to pinpoint the real and active ones.

Jake reached for his coffee and was about to take a sip when one of the building's side doors burst open, and a dark-haired woman in a hospital gown spilled out, tumbling onto the crumbling asphalt the moment she crossed the threshold. She frantically looked around, her eyes wide, as she used her hands to right herself and return to her feet. She looked his way momentarily before taking off in the opposite direction, running toward the waving corn behind the building.

Jake spilled his drink, trying to shove it back into the cupholder—at least it was cold at this point in the stakeout—while reaching for his phone. Before he had a chance to dial into headquarters and report the sighting, a garage door attached to the warehouse opened, and a Jeep slowly edged out. The lab-coat-clad man driving the Jeep didn't look worried as he turned toward the field, as though he knew the woman's location and felt he could take his time catching her. *Tracking device,* Jake surmised, shaking his head. *That poor woman.*

The moment his call was answered, he filled in his handler. "There's definitely an illegal lab here. I'm heading into the field to help a woman who just escaped. Send backup, and let's take this facility down." Jake hung up before they could instruct him to remain in place. His mission was reconnaissance-only, but the woman's terrified face was burned into his brain, and every part of him was pulled toward saving her.

It wasn't like she'd be the first FUC-rescued lab patient. At this point, half of the occupancy at the FUCN'A—Furry United Coalition Newbie Academy—was made up of lab escapees or evacuees who were acclimating to their new abilities.

Jake waited for just a few heartbeats, making sure no one else emerged from the warehouse, before hopping out of the SUV. He fought the urge to shift into his fox, as he had no idea if there were any human bystanders nearby or about to drive past. Shifting in front of humans meant a mountain of paperwork to complete, documenting why he shifted and how many possible human witnesses there were, such as the COOCHI—Corrective Outdoor-shift Or Calming of Humans Incident—form. It was needed before each instance where FUC had to create cover stories for the event, such as a "gas leak" that caused hallucinations. And even then, it was becoming more and more difficult for FUC to contain events, thanks to camera phones and videos instantly posted all over social media.

So, he avoided the hassle and entered the field in his human form, which at least still offered him an enhanced sense of smell. The aroma of dried cornstalks mingled with the woman's aroma, though his heart broke when he realized how much of her scent was pure fear. *Hang in there,* he hoped for her. *You're out now, and that's better than the alternative. Now, I'm going to find you and take you away from this hell.*

Bent golden shafts showed Jake the woman's path. He jogged through the maze, almost taking an ear to the junk as the stalks whipped around. Her path through was dizzying, proof that the hapless woman was disoriented and running in circles, which made his task difficult. He had to figure out where she was, and fast. The scientist had a head start.

He slowed at a large imprint in the mud, where it seemed she must have fallen, and then his ears pricked up at the sound of talking ahead. He couldn't make out what was being said before the timbre of a man's voice—likely the man in the lab coat—was cut off by a screech that ripped through Jake's ear drums like a banshee's cry. The sound dropped him to his knees, and his hands flew to his head, despite it being too late to protect his hearing. The residual ringing deafened him from the rest of the world and made his head feel like it pulsed, but he forced himself back to his feet.

He couldn't give up. He had to find the woman.

Nearby, a murder of crows took to flight, and Jake ran as fast as he could in that direction, hoping their movement was an indication of the woman's new location. He knew he was on the right track when he found a new set of disturbed stalks, and as he followed the path, the woman's scent grew stronger.

Her fear mingled with the dry smell of autumn, dancing on the cool breeze, a pleasantness that stirred something inside of him that he didn't have time to examine while he fiercely searched for her.

He reached the edge of the field, where the golden corn glowed orange from the setting sun, and he finally found her.

In a ditch. On her hands and knees, clutching her side while retching.

The run probably took a toll on her body.

Jake slowly approached, looking her over for injury. He saw no blood, but her tangled, dark hair mingled with the wet grass, clumps of mud clinging to it as she dry-heaved. The lack of substance coming out of her was no surprise. If this lab operated as others had, they wouldn't feed their specimens much.

A gruesome fact that Jake remembered from his own past experiences.

Jake had seen many horrific experiments from the labs over the years. Some of them kept him up at night. Especially knowing that not all of the shifters adjusted to their changes… or the trauma. Thinking about it all hit too close to home.

Jake moved forward, hoping to comfort the woman, but he stopped dead in his tracks when she snapped her head up and glared at him as she rose to her feet. Her hospital gown flopped around in the breeze, but

Jake didn't let his eyes wander. Her pale lips moved, but her the sound was muffled to him. He pointed at his ear and shook his head to signal that he couldn't hear. Her wide green eyes, glittering emeralds set in the dark skin of her face, were full of fear when she started pointing, thrusting her finger forward in a stabbing motion.

Jake finally realized that she wasn't pointing *at* him but *behind* him. He whirled around to come face to face with the man in the white lab coat.

The man raised his arm and drove a taser right at Jake's chest.

Paige had moved until her body refused to go any further and her legs buckled, giving in to the stress of running. Her ribs burned, and her stomach expelled nothing but bile into the ditch. Her knees sank into the moist ground as she spewed.

Just my luck, Paige thought as a shadow fell over her. She readied herself for the taser jolt and wondered why the scientist was hesitating. After all, she'd practically burst his eardrums—however the hell she'd managed to make that sound—so she imagined he was probably pretty pissed at her. He'd probably kick it up a notch, just to make her pay.

But Paige looked up to find a Mr. Tall-Dark-and-Handsome instead—a man she'd never seen before. His calming scent reminded her of the woods of her childhood. The cool wind tousled his dark hair, ruffling it in a way that, combined with his bewildered yet determined look, reminded her of a certain fictional FBI agent chasing after lights in the sky.

He didn't hold a taser or make a move to grab her, but the suit he wore was enough to warn her off. Paige had learned long ago not to trust men in suits. No matter how hot they looked.

"What the hell are you waiting for?" she quipped, hoping he'd give her some long lecture that would give her enough time to find the strength to bolt again.

His brows furrowed in confusion. Paige cocked her head to the side, trying to decide if this man was real or a hallucination. If he was real, why wasn't he moving against her? After all the time she'd been held captive in the lab, had psychosis finally crept in? When the man motioned toward his ears, Paige realized he must have been affected by her powerful scream, as the scientist had been.

Behind the new attractive man, the lab-coat-clad scientist emerged from the corn. She noted the way Dr. Green assessed Mr. Suit and confirmed they weren't on the same team when he pointed his taser at the new man. She tried to warn Mr. Suit, motioning with her hands for him to turn around. *He's clearly not the brightest,* she thought, as it took him seemingly forever to finally understand and turn to face his would-be assailant. Paige tensed, sure Mr. Suit would be a goner.

To her surprise, the hottie moved with lightning-fast speed, graciously sidestepping the wires that sprang from the taser when Dr. Green pulled the trigger. Moving as elegantly as a dancer, Mr. Suit swooped back behind the evil scientist, sweeping him into his arms and straight into a chokehold.

Finally, Paige thought, *one of the men who poked, prodded, and starved me is getting a taste of his own medicine.* Paige watched with excitement, her heart thudding in her chest as Dr. Green's knees gave out and his eyes rolled back in his head. He began to lose consciousness just as black crept into the corners of her own vision.

Muffled sounds hit her ears, and she vaguely realized she was slipping away. She'd pushed her body to the limit in her escape, and now it was shoving back.

Paige passed out, once again helpless to prevent whatever atrocity awaited her.

2

Paige awoke in a soft bed with a pounding headache. The machines beeping around her didn't help.

She opened her eyes, glancing down at her garb and sighing as her vision cleared and she realized her situation had not improved. She still wore a hospital gown, her freedom elusive. She swiveled her head on her sore neck to take in her surroundings, assessing that her location looked much different from any of the lab facilities she'd been kept in. In addition to the soft bed and the beeping machines, the room also held a bedside chair and table with a vase of flowers. Instead of a large glass observation wall, the room had a window that let the sunshine stream in and gave her a view of the lush greenery outside.

Paige had gotten used to expecting the worst, but her mood lightened when she realized her wrists were free—not shackled to the bed! So far, it seemed like she was in an upgraded location. *Could I be in a proper hospital? Or did the hottie in the suit take me to his lab?*

Was he some freak billionaire who liked to keep pets?

No. His suit was nice, but it hadn't been *billionaire* nice. It looked more like something a government official or someone of that sort might wear. The thought did not ease her mind any. Being a government captive wasn't any better than being a private captive. Paige definitely did not want to trade one type of imprisonment for another. This tiger was sick of being in a zoo.

She looked from the port in her hand to the pole next to the bed with the bag of fluids. Whatever it dripped into her was cool—a much different tingle in her veins than the one that had burned her in the lab for so long. She closed her eyes, exploring her mind and finding the barriers that had been put in before were gone. Her tiger stirred as though it was part of her again. She could shift—she was certain of it. Her cat-side had been freed of its mental shackles.

She'd almost feel like she was back to her *old self* if what happened in the cornfield didn't still haunt her. Something new had occurred when she screamed, and it scared her. That sound hadn't been human, and it wasn't quite animal either. *What the hell did they do to me?* Paige's mind raced, but she couldn't access most of her memories. They were either fuzzy or just...missing. It was an uncomfortable feeling. Pieces of her earlier childhood were there, but then the rest was blank.

Refusing to become complacent and unsure of who to trust, Paige eased the IV out. Whoever her captors were, she wasn't about to pump who knows what into her body. Especially when no one asked for her opinion first. Holding the needle in her hand brought back a memory of her dad holding her hand while she received vaccines as a child. She could smell the musky scent of his aftershave so strong that she could have sworn she could turn to see him in the room next to her. Paige hated needles back then, and she loathed them more now. She wanted nothing more than her dad's callused hands wrapped around hers, telling her it would all be all right.

She sat up, swinging her legs over the side of the bed and sliding down until her heels pressed into the cool linoleum. Blackness fuzzed the outer edges of her vision, and the walls blurred around her. She'd sat up too quickly.

The physical activity from her earlier escape had taken a toll on her body. *Especially considering I'd basically been starved.* She tapped her feet on the ground and took a few deep breaths as she waited for her head to clear.

When she felt steady enough, she eased off the bed, testing her weight on her legs. When her knees didn't buckle and her head didn't spin, Paige crept toward the door opposite her bed.

She cracked the door open and peered around, squinting as she took in her new surroundings. To one side, a couple of chatty nurses faced away from her at a desk, not appearing to notice Paige eyeing them. A stack of charts overflowed from the bin on the corner of their counter, adding to the appearance that she was in a normal hospital. Even so, she wasn't about to take any chances.

She glanced the other way, finding the hall empty other than a monitor mounted on the wall. Paige crept a little farther out of her room, and when no one stopped her, she swiftly stepped into the hall and headed away from the nurses. If she had any luck, she'd be out of this place and on her way to safety in no time.

Paige padded silently on bare feet, holding her hospital gown closed behind her.

No one yelled at her to stop. Had the nurses been too distracted to notice she was out of her room, or was this just one more lab-supervised test, like her last escape?

Despite her suspicions, the relief of freedom swelled in her chest, mingling with hope, emotions she'd thought she'd never have again after what felt like a lifetime of captivity.

Which were quickly dashed as she rounded a corner just to bounce off of the chest of Mr. Tall-Dark-and-Handsome.

Jake's mind was a whirlwind of thoughts. For starters, he couldn't get the look of the woman's eyes out of his head. The fear in them beckoned to him. He wanted—no, he needed—to soothe her and let her know that everything would be all right. But behind the fear, something ferocious lurked.

It had captivated him.

As a field agent, Jake wasn't supposed to befriend the shifters he rescued. His job was over once he safely delivered them to a FUC facility and handed them over to the experts who would rehabilitate them. Yet, he wasn't ready to leave the green-eyed beauty behind. He needed to know that she was okay.

Which was why he found himself at the WANC—the Working and Administration Networking Core, FUCN'A's main building—strolling through the hospital wing for the woman. His animal side yearned to comfort the cornered animal he saw at the edge of the cornfield. No creature deserved to feel the way that woman did. He could sense her raw panic. Her confusion and anger. He wanted to assure her that he'd protect her. Find out her story.

See her eyes filled with anything other than that primal dread.

He knew it wouldn't be easy, though. Someone in her situation wouldn't open up to just anyone. Which is why he imagined the words he'd say over and over in his head like he was reviewing lines for a play. Nervousness bubbled in his stomach, a feeling reminiscent of summoning the courage to ask a classmate in high school to prom. The closer he made it to the woman's room, the more his anxiety gnawed at him. He was wondering if he should change his mind when he approached a corner and the woman faceplanted into his chest.

He reached for her, gripping her shoulders to steady her. "Shouldn't you be in bed?" Jake wanted to smack himself on the forehead. *Way to sound like a complete dork.* Jake had envisioned himself being far more charming.

She yanked free from his grasp, and he was glad to see her green eyes no longer tainted by fear. She looked him up and down with calm and confidence—and perhaps a tinge of anger—before answering, "I don't know. No one told me to. Are you about to inform me that you're my doctor and order me back to bed?"

"No. I am not your doctor," he replied, looking down at his suit and wondering if any doctors dressed in such a way.

"My captor then? About to tase me and drag me back to my cell?"

"No, not that either," he replied, fumbling as he lost all of his planned lines. *This conversation is not going as planned.* Any hope that the woman would swoon over her rescuer completely faded. "Sorry. Let me start again. Maybe with an introduction? I'm Agent Park. Uh... Jake. I work for the Fury United Coalition, and I'm the lead agent for the team that raided the lab where you'd been kept." He squared up his shoulders as he spoke. Jake was proud of his role at FUC and thrilled to be in a position to help the shifter community.

The woman before him didn't seem to share the sentiment. She crossed her arms, appearing not at all impressed. "The Fury United Coalition…" she mused, looking off in the distance as though trying to place where she may have heard the term before.

"FUC. We protect our kind," he explained softly. "Now, would you be willing to tell me your name?"

"I'm Paige," she answered, re-focusing her eyes on him with a determined set of her jaw. "And I demand you tell me where I am."

"You're somewhere safe now," Jake said, tilting his head and offering her a small smile.

Paige squinted as if trying to read his mind. "That's a vague answer that doesn't really tell me anything."

"You're at a FUC facility—our Canadian academy, actually. Future cadets are trained here, but we also rehabilitate shifters like yourself. Ones who've been through a bad time and need some healing."

"Why should I believe you?" she asked, raising an eyebrow. Skepticism left her second-guessing everything. It was safer to stay on edge, expecting the worst instead of being caught unaware again.

"You can leave at any time. We just suggest that you take time to get used to any new abilities before you do."

Paige's arms finally dropped, hanging limp at her sides. Her shoulders rolled forward as if she felt defeated. Her eyes glanced to the floor. "Do you know what they did to me?"

Jake didn't know what to say. He felt so stupid for going out of his way to see her again, as though he'd be able to impress her. *I should have stayed in my lane. Let the doctors help her and just picked up my next mission and moved on.* She had so much going on, and Jake had been busy thinking about himself and how he felt instead of what might have been best for her. "I am sorry; I don't. But we have a team of doctors and scientists who can help you to figure that out."

Her black tangled hair blanketed her face before she attempted to push it behind her ear and then looked up at him, her face expressionless for a moment. "I don't need more scientists poking me with needles and throwing me in machines."

She wobbled a little, and he worried she might collapse again, as she had in the cornfield. He reached out, cupping her elbow. "Steady there."

Instead of thanking him, she pushed his chest, making him drop her arm and take a step back. "I don't need *you*!" she snapped, her eyebrows pushed up in anger as her eyes widened. Before Jake could say another word, Paige turned on her heel and marched back around the corner.

3

Paige shuffled back into her hospital room, forgetting about finding a way out of the facility while focusing on wanting nothing more than to distance herself from Agent Jake Park. She shut the door and punched the wall, willing herself to forget the way he looked at her and how good it felt to have his hand on her arm, supporting her.

She couldn't remember a time when she had someone in her life like that. All she could remember was the way the lab personnel looked at her like she was a lab rat to be studied. Their eyes had held a sick curiosity only, while Agent Jake Park's held a soft caring that suggested he wanted to help her.

Paige's legs gave out, and she crumpled to the floor. She hugged her knees to chest as hot tears spilled down her face. She wanted to get the hell out of there and go home, but she couldn't remember home. Not where it was, not who it included, like her family. Nothing. She couldn't even say if she lived in an apartment or a house. Paige remembered what FUC was, but that didn't ease her mind any. How did she know she could trust them? Just because they thought they were the good guys didn't mean that they had her best intentions at heart.

She rocked back and forth, soothing herself as she often did in her cells. The calm eventually started to wash over her just as the door opened. She kept her forehead pressed to her knees as she said, "Agent Jake, if you've come to tell me how great this place is, you can cram it up your ass."

But the person who walked in didn't have the same woodsy smell that Jake did. Instead, her visitor smelled more like fresh rain and flowers, and her voice was just as soft and calming. "Hello there, Paige. I'm Dr. Brown. You can stay there if you want."

Paige sniffed, wiping her nose on her arm and daring a glance up at the woman whose kind face smiled at Paige. She threw the long braid of her dark hair over her shoulder as she adjusted the stethoscope that hung around her neck like a sleeping snake. "Are you here to inject me with something?" Paige's voice quivered. She was well over playing guinea pig for people.

"No," Dr. Brown said as she took a seat in the lone chair in the room, offering Paige a smile that didn't reach her tired eyes. Dark circles showed through her makeup as if she had little sleep lately. "But I am here to talk to you about your situation."

"How long was I out for?" Paige asked, unsure as to when she was rescued.

"Agent Park brought you in two days ago. You were clearly exhausted and malnourished, hence the IV drip. We also wanted to make sure we treated you for any non-obvious conditions, so we did take a blood sample." Paige was about to protest that she never gave them permission to do that when Dr. Brown added, "We have to do it to screen for anomalies to ensure your safety and the safety of others here at the Academy."

Paige shuddered. If she ever ran into one of the lab scientists again, she didn't know what sort of evil thing she would do to them. But whatever it was, she felt deeply that they would deserve it. "What does my bloodwork show?"

"It appears some of your genes were modified, and it will take us some time to break it all down." Dr. Brown looked at her tablet before adding, "We have identified one modified genetic marker that we are not familiar with, but we can tell it affects your vocal cords."

"Yes!" Paige practically shouted as she peeled herself up off the floor, remembering the man from the lab in the cornfield and how his ears bled. "Something weird happened when I screamed in the cornfield."

"Did it hurt you?" The doctor scribbled something on her tablet.

"No. But it hurt one of the men who experimented on me." She detailed the whole cornfield experience, including the blood from Lab Coat's ears. *We have to do it to screen for anomalies to ensure your safety and the safety of others here at the Academy.* Dr. Brown's words made more sense now. It was one thing to harm someone who was trying to capture her, but she didn't want it to happen to innocent people. The thought of hurting someone who was trying to help her was unbearable.

A voice in the back of her mind nagged, *But what if they aren't here to help?* She pushed the thought away, making the choice to trust Dr. Brown.

"That must have been a startling experience," Dr. Brown said, still writing on her tablet. "If it's not too difficult to think about, can you tell me what you remember about the lab itself, both the personnel and what they did to you?"

Paige nodded and tried to remember every detail she could and explain it to the doctor. As she did, memories of her horrific time at the lab flooded her brain. Like waves on the beach, they washed over her, each one more painful than the last, forcing her to take gasping breaths to continue. But Paige pushed on, recounting her experiences to the doctor.

The doctor intently listened to every word Paige

said as she listed off the tests they made her endure and the machine they would sometimes hook her up to. She hated that. The giant round disk that spanned from the floor to the ceiling of the tiled room behind her stunk of burnt circuits. It was a metal iris designed to bring another world closer. Circuits and crystals spread across the surface of it like lichen on a rock. The scientists had connected all sorts of cords and cables that ran across the floor like arteries that were supposed to bring the contraption to life. Paige was thought to be its spark of life, though that never made sense to her. The delusional Dr. Green chained her inside some sort of a chamber, activating a testing sequence so painful Paige always feared she wouldn't survive another round in there. Between the cold metal of her bindings, biting into the skin of her wrists, and the shocks they would give her if she didn't comply, Paige didn't know how much more she could take. And each time they pulled her out, the scientist seemed disappointed, though she had no idea what results they'd hoped to obtain.

Throughout the session, Dr. Brown handed her tissues and let her take her time with the details. When Paige finally felt she'd told her everything, she added, "I can't remember things from before the lab. And I'm not sure if I even remember everything they did to me in there."

Dr. Brown gave her a tight-lipped, sympathetic look. "You're not the first one to say that. So far, we've not discovered if the memory loss is intentional or if it's a side effect of the trauma."

"Will I get my memory back?"

"Some have, some haven't, unfortunately." Dr. Brown appeared sad as she revealed the truth.

There went any hope that FUC had a magical serum to restore her memory. "So what happens now?"

"You can stay here, in the dormitories, as long as you need, since you don't remember where your home is. We'll contact different tiger prides to see if we can track down your family. If we can find who you belong to, you can go home with them. However, we do keep in touch with those we rescue to ensure they're in control of any new abilities."

She didn't need to say more than that. Paige could imagine how bad it would be if she let out a damaging scream in the middle of a crowded mall or something. "So you'll keep doing tests?"

"We have your bloodwork on file, and any further testing will only be done with your consent," she assured as she stood. "Now, a nurse will bring you some clothes to change into before you're escorted to the dormitories. Now that your speedy shifter healing has returned, you shouldn't need any more treatment here in the clinic wing, but if you need anything, we're here for you."

Paige nodded, not knowing what else to say. The doctor smiled warmly before exiting the room and leaving Paige alone with her thoughts.

The new silence of the room felt unbearable. Soon it filled with the dull sounds around her as Paige focused her hearing. Sounds Paige had forgotten when her shifter powers and senses were dulled with drugs in the lab, such as the footsteps of the doctor retreating softly down the hall. The sound was as gentle as the woman's voice and demeanor had been, and it filled Paige with a calm that she had not known for some time. She'd been so used to being on edge that she found it difficult to relax, but she tried to remain hopeful that this place would be different. It wasn't just some no-name government agency buried in shadow.

Now that she was no longer stuck in a lab, she could focus on her new reality, such as why some memories had stuck with her, but others didn't. Why could she recall her name and FUC but not her family's? Paige chewed the edge of her pinky fingernail—the only one out of the ten that hadn't already been gnawed to the quick—as uneasiness bubbled within, churning her stomach. She was trying to trust Dr. Brown, but it just wasn't that easy to shake what she'd been through. Look at what had happened in the cornfield. She'd thought she was free, but it had been just another test. This could be part of the lab's plan too. An elaborate ploy to make her feel safe and drop her guard...

Paige glared at the door, narrowing her eyes and backing up against the wall as new footsteps approached. After a quick knock, a woman in scrubs entered. “Hello, I’ve brought you some clothes,” the nurse said in a high-pitched voice with a large smile across her face as she placed a pile of fabric on the bed. “They should fit, but if not, please let one of us know. Someone will be down in about ten minutes to escort you up to the dorms to meet your roommate.”

Her cheerfulness made anger swell in the pit of Paige’s core. The nurse must have noticed because she quickly turned on her heel and left the room. The door clicked shut behind her.

Paige approached the bed, eyeing the clothes suspiciously as if they might attack at any moment. She picked up the nondescript sweatpants, T-shirt, and undergarments and wanted to scream. She wanted to take the clothes and throw them into the hall. Or better yet, light them on fire and watch them burn.

She squeezed the fabric tight in her hands and suddenly wanted to cry again. Why was she so uneasy? So emotional? It was hard for her to keep up with her moods. She felt like she would split apart at any moment into a pile of flesh and gore. Part of her hoped it would happen so that this nightmare would end.

A knock on the door brought Paige out of her thoughts. “Just a minute!” she shouted, louder than expected. Her tiger growled in her throat, ready to erupt and pounce on the unexpecting target at her door.

She pushed aside her emotions and dressed quickly, tossing the hospital gown onto the bed. She looked around. She had no personal belongings to gather, which felt odd. Surely in her old life, she would have at least had a purse or cell phone to grab.

Shrugging it off, she opened the door.

A familiar face greeted her, like a bad penny she couldn't lose. "I offered to show you up to your room."

The words flew from his mouth before Jake knew what he was saying. After his last embarrassing encounter with Paige, he wanted a do-over, but so far, he wasn't off on the right foot. *Why does she leave me tongue-tied?*

Jake assumed a familiar face would ease the transition for Paige, but after hearing her growl through the door, he wondered if his instincts were wrong.

I shouldn't allow myself to get involved, he thought, though it was too late. It wasn't just that he'd personally rescued Paige. It was that the whole situation reminded him of his own past.

Part of the reason Jake became a FUC agent was because his own mother had been a rescued shifter. It took a long time for her to adjust after coming home from rehabilitation. Jake was only ten years old when she disappeared. The day his mother returned home was the happiest of his lifeuntil he realized she wasn't the same person anymore. He'd wake up from a dead sleep, her screams from down the hall ringing in his ears. Her nightmares seemed to occur every night, and from his bedroom, Jake could hear his father trying to calm her down as she whimpered, recounting the details of the dream.

It took years of counseling before his mom could sleep through the night. Most of the time, she was his old mom again, but sometimes a noise or a scent would wake something in her, and she'd be that cornered animal again. But as quick as it would come, she would sigh and close her eyes, pretending nothing was wrong. But Jake could see it still affected her.

But for all the shifters Jake rescued, Paige was the first he'd felt a connection with. His past missions involved batch rescues, with the prisoners clinging to each other for support. He hadn't felt they were isolated and alone like Paige had been.

Was that it? Would he feel less compelled toward her once she had a solid support system of other rescued experiments?

Part of him hoped so because that meant he could focus back on his work.

Another part of him hoped not because he wanted Paige in his life for some reason.

"Are you ready to go?" he asked and then thought twice. "If you'd be more comfortable with someone else, I can get one of the nurses to—"

"No," she cut him off, and he was glad to see the angles of her face soften, and her muscles relax. "I'd rather have you."

The simple phrase made his heart swell, though he

knew she didn't mean it in the intimate way it felt. "Okay," he replied.

Paige glanced around the room one last time before softly asking, "Is this what my new room will look like?"

"No. It will look more like a college dorm. And you will have a roommate."

"Who's my roommate?" The light shimmered in her long lashes as she blinked up at him.

Jake swallowed, trying to gather his thoughts. "I'm not sure. But we can find out together," he said, offering her a wide smile. For the first time, Paige smiled back.

It melted his heart.

4

Mr. Tall-Dark-and-Handsome isn't all that *bad,* Paige thought to herself as she followed him out of the hospital wing and toward an elevator. *He's certainly more tolerable than the super cheerful nurse.*

Plus, he'd said he *offered* to give her a tour and show her to her new room, which meant that he was choosing to be around her. She wasn't making it easy for him, yet he came back to check in on her. It could be that this agent kept tabs on every shifter he rescued, but Paige didn't think so. Jake genuinely seemed to care about how she was adjusting. Her heart begged her to ease up a little, to give him a chance, despite the fear that ran like an undercurrent inside of her.

"The real heart of FUCN'A is outside the massive WANC," Jake explained, leading Paige to the glass doors that led to the rest of the campus. The outdoors blossomed with chirping birds and the grunts of cadets as they plunged through the obstacle course. A bouncing woman with cascading blonde curls was smiling with words of encouragement that sounded more like threats to Paige. "You'll only get your license to FUC if you show your worth on the training fields! A good FUC needs all of your heart and soul. Now give it to me!" The woman twitched her nose as she followed some of the cadets along the side of the course, all while nibbling on a small piece of what looked like carrot cake.

Paige couldn't help but notice how different the cadets looked from those she encountered in the hospital wing. Their figures were full, and they appeared healthy and full of energy. And there was one stark difference—she could see no deformities on any of them. While in the hospital wing, Paige overheard all sorts of chatter from the nurses about a woman with scales, a man whose teeth resembled needles and couldn't close his mouth, and even another woman with a horn protruding from her forehead. Paige couldn't even imagine what that nightmare must be like. She may have been experimented on, but she still appeared normal. The thought actually caused a pang of guilt. Survivor's guilt, maybe. It left her wondering why she didn't end up with a physical abnormality.

"Do you give tours to every shifter you rescue?" Paige asked, her heart beating rapidly from not being used to the exertion of walking. She felt like a wimp for being out of breath on a leisurely stroll.

Jake's dark brows scrunched up as he thought for a moment. "No. I usually don't." His soft voice was honey to Paige's ears. It put her mind at ease.

Paige let the comment hang in the air. Not knowing how to respond, she instead inquired, "How many were at the lab where I was kept? I never saw any of them but could sometimes hear whimpering late at night."

Jake's spikey hair fluttered as he shook his head. "You were the only one recovered in the raid. They must have moved the others before we raided the place."

Her mind churned as she pulled on a dry piece of skin on her lip. *Did my imagination make up the whimpers?* She wondered, doubting her own sanity.

"There appeared to be other cells there, but they were all empty," Jake added as if sensing Paige needed clarification.

She nodded slowly. Remembering her situation slowly was becoming overwhelming. Her hands shook as she tried to push the memories from her mind and change the conversation to a new topic. "What got you into FUC in the first place?"

"My mom," Jake said as the shouts of the training field became echoes in the distance as they neared a beautiful lake. "I guess I know how painful it can be for a family to heal from shifter experimentation."

Paige felt there was more to the story, but Jake didn't offer up any additional personal tidbits.

"Is this the lake?" She wanted to kick herself for such a dumb question, but Jake didn't comment on the obviousness of it. Instead, he nodded as his dark eyes peered out across the smooth surface of the water, seemingly lost in thought.

"It's beautiful," Paige added, smiling as a flock of geese floated near the shore, bobbing their heads under periodically to scour for food.

She stood with Jake in silence at the edge of the water, enjoying the peace and the pleasantness of the sun reflecting off the surface. For a moment, Paige felt at home—safe with Jake at her side. She practically forgot about the monstrosities she had been through, simply relaxing in his company. It was a light, wonderful feeling.

"I should get you back," he said, cutting through the quiet.

The cadets were off the course by the time they walked back past, toward WANC. The brick of the building was a sharp contrast to the green campus surrounding it. Its height cut into the perfect blue sky. Paige wondered how they were able to keep it all secret from the humans over the years. She'd learned that, to outsiders, FUCN'A was the Animal Rescue Special House of Learning, or ARSHOL Paige hoped to learn who came up with these acronyms.

Their walk back was silent. What energy she'd felt

before the walk had been depleted. Jake led her through the doors of the lobby, where they started their tour, and he ushered her into the elevator.

As the doors shuddered shut, Paige sighed. "I'm sorry for earlier." She kept her eyes on the floor, ashamed of how she'd acted. She might not know many details about her previous life, but she felt certain that the anger inside her now was completely new. Alien. An unwanted guest who refused to leave.

It concerned her even more that the anger seemed to be winding itself around her tiger, slowly stitching itself to her animal side and creating a divide between human and beast. The tiger's instincts were to alert her to any form of danger, no matter how improbable. It wanted to protect her, but Paige felt it was too reactionary and on-edge, seeing everything and everyone as a possible threat.

The thought sent a shiver up Paige's spine.

Shifters were supposed to be at one with their animal side, that much she knew for sure. She didn't need to remember things from her past to know that when human and animal weren't interconnected, something was terribly wrong. She felt unbalanced.

If the anger took root in her shifter side, she could become enraged and out of control.

"There's nothing to be sorry for. You've been through a lot," Jake said, causing Paige to glance up at him. His brown eyes were warm and comforting. His brow furrowed as if he battled with some painful memory. Paige wanted to ask what was wrong, but the elevator *dinged,* and the doors creaked open. "Please follow me," he said, ushering her into the hallway.

Doors flanked them, but the atmosphere wasn't cold and sterile like back at the lab or even the hospital wing. Laughter from one of the rooms tickled her ears —a sound she almost forgot existed. It fostered the hope growing inside of her, signaling that this place maybe *was* different.

Jake stopped at one of the doors and knocked softly. It creaked open a few inches. A face hid in the shadows from within. Paige could barely make out the features in the darkness. "I'm escorting up your new roommate," Jake explained. The door swung open, seemingly by itself, as the figure within couldn't be seen from the hall.

Jake turned to Paige. "Do you want me to go in first?"

Paige nodded. She wasn't sure she was ready to meet anyone new. In fact, she wanted to run the other way down the hall. But she reminded herself that her roommate was someone just like her who had been rescued from a lab somewhere. They were the same—both broken people who needed a friend.

With that in mind, Paige took a breath and eased her way into the dark chamber.

A bit of sunlight peeked in from around a blanket that covered the window. The small dark figure rushed to the window and peeled the blanket off, dropping it to the floor in a crumpled pile. "Sorry. They never shut the lights off where I was, so now I take all the dark I can get." The woman shrugged, her shoulders touching the bottoms of her blonde bob. She turned her round face to Paige, a wide smile on her face. "I should have been ready for you. They told me this morning I had a roommate." Her tiny frame was swallowed up by the sweatsuit she wore. Paige noted how skinny the woman was when she crossed her arms.

"I'm Ellie." As she reached out her hand, shadows appeared to spill off of her arm in clouds that evaporated before Paige's eyes. "I hope my…uh…side effects don't make you uncomfortable. It's some sort of dark matter waves refracting light through the lens of my skin…or whatever." Her voice trailed off as she dropped her eyes to the floor. "It's kind of above my pay grade. I just know it looks weird." She shrugged.

"It doesn't bother me at all," Paige said, taking Ellie's hand to shake. "I'm Paige."

Ellie eyed up Jake suspiciously. Her blonde eyebrows seemingly squeezed her eyes shut as she did so. "I'm Agent Park, and I really should be going. Hopefully, I can run into you later, Paige." He voiced it as if it were a question.

"I would like that," Paige replied.

Jake smiled before turning to leave, shutting the door quietly behind him.

"How did *you* get an agent escort, and where do I

find mine?" Ellie joked as a wide smile broke across her pale face.

Paige explained, "He was the one who found me. I guess he wanted to check in on me."

"Lucky," Ellie replied. "That's unusual. It's not routine for the rescuing agent to check in on the shifters at FUCN'A."

Paige couldn't complain. "His heart seems to be in the right place. Having a familiar face escort me to my room felt nice."

"Plus, he's easy on the eyes," Ellie added, flopping onto her bed in a way that made Paige feel like they were at a slumber party talking about a cute boy.

"I guess." Paige smiled, not admitting to Ellie how much she loved the way his black hair spiked up playfully in the front or how attractive she found the way his muscular shoulders filled out his suit.

Now that Paige thought about it, Jake was sexy as hell.

A finger snap brought her back to reality. "Paige! Come back from those dreams about the handsome Agent Park!" Ellie smirked while crossing her ankles. Paige watched as the shadows floated off her in dark clouds again before vanishing.

"Sorry," Paige replied, not bothering to deny it as she ran a hand over her new bed and dresser, marveling at how nice they were versus her cells at the lab.

"How long have you known him? When did you get

here? Have you always been a shifter?" The words tumbled out of Ellie's mouth before Paige had a chance to respond to any of the questions. Ellie paused for a moment, biting her lip. "Sorry. There's not much entertainment around here, and I've been kept kind of isolated for a while."

"That's okay," Paige said with a sympathetic smile. "I can start from the beginning. From what I can remember anyway." Paige eased onto her new bed and told her story, ending with Jake taking her to the dorms.

Ellie stared with wide eyes. "So you've been a shifter your whole life?" she asked after a moment, her voice soft and timid.

"Yeah. Except the ear-piercing scream is new." Paige rubbed her throat at the unsettling thought of someone augmenting or changing her DNA. "What about you?"

"No." Ellie's voice was thick with tears as she stared at the floor. "This is *all* new to me."

Paige almost fell off her bed in shock at Ellie's admission. She couldn't imagine what it must be like for Ellie to go her whole life not knowing shifters existed until she was turned into one. "You must have been so confused when they first rescued you." Paige didn't know what else to say. All the lines she thought of dried up in her throat for fear that she would make Ellie feel worse.

The worry must have shown on Paige's face because Ellie quickly blurted out, "I guess it's not so bad." She held her hand in front of her face, squinting as if in a trance as she watched the shadows roll off the palm of her hand.

"What are they?" Paige finally asked.

Ellie looked up from the dancing black smoke. "Not sure." As she closed her hand, the dark clouds evaporated. "But I've invented a word to describe it."

"Do you mean shifting?" Paige cocked her head to the side, wondering what Ellie was referring to.

"No." Ellie laughed darkly. "My hybrid ability. I call it shadow-walking."

Before Paige could ask more, Ellie disappeared off the bed. Paige looked around the room, trying to figure out where her roommate disappeared to. The shadow cast from the edge of the bed elongated, sprouting up as if an invisible tree appeared in the middle of the room to create it. The blackness slowly took anthropomorphic form. Paige stared at the head and watched as the features began to take shape and color as if an unseen artist were painting the image before her eyes. It was Ellie coming back into existence.

"Whoa!" Paige shouted in amazement. "That is amazing!"

Ellie beamed a satisfied smile at her. "It takes a bit of practice, and at first, I was incredibly anxious I would disappear forever, but I like the feeling better than shifting."

"What animal do you change into?"

Ellie snorted. "A black cat."

"What's wrong with that?" Paige asked, slightly offended on behalf of her tiger side.

"Nothing, I guess." Ellie crossed the room back to her bed and plopped back down onto the mattress. "It's just not as exciting as teleporting. Well, actually, that's not what I do. It's been explained to me that I bend light differently. But as I said before, it's above my paygrade. And way too much explaining." She giggled at the thought, shaking her head.

Paige bit her lip, her head spinning from the trials of the lab. It felt like trying to get your sea legs. "Do you remember anything from before you were changed?"

She pursed her lips as she thought. "I remember basic things. My name, for one. That I was fully human, for another. Oh, and I don't like beans. But everything else..."

"Gone," Paige finished for her, her heart sinking as she said it.

Ellie glanced at the clock on the wall. "You want to come to lunch with me? I can show you around afterward if you want."

Paige wanted to ask Ellie so much more about her rescue, especially what else she remembered from her previous life, but she held back. While Ellie kept a chipper demeanor, Paige could sense that Ellie was not as well-adjusted as she let on. The thought pained Paige and made her remember all the scientists who experimented on her against her will. She had a hard time coming to terms with knowing similar things had happened to so many others.

"Why did they do this to us?" she asked, not realizing she said it aloud.

"I don't know," Ellie said. "But I hope to one day make them sorry they did."

5

Jake hummed to himself as he waltzed back to the meeting room, his mind replaying the way the light danced in Paige's green eyes when he talked to her. His heart was a flutter just thinking about it, and he couldn't deny wanting to spend more time with Paige —both to know her better and make sure that he could protect her.

But she wasn't the only thing on his mind as he walked into the makeshift war room. Something bothered him about the lab. Jake couldn't stand the idea that someone might be out-foxing him. No matter how many labs he helped to break up, there were more out there. And the lab organizers always seemed to be one step ahead of them—in the wind before FUC could arrive on the scene. It drove him crazy. Especially after Paige noted she heard others at night. Where did they go?

"Here are the lab photos, Agent Park," One of the junior agents held up a folder as he entered the commandeered meeting room.

Jake thanked him and picked up the file, preferring to have a physical printout to pin to the wall rather than paging through digital files on his tablet. Something else plagued his mind. Dr. Brown's notes from her meeting with Paige mentioned a machine, and Jake couldn't connect the description to anything they found in the facility they raided. *Were they taking her to another site?* he wondered as he perused the photographs for hints. *Or had they somehow managed to dismantle things before they were raided?* None of the rooms in the lab resembled the chamber or machine she mentioned to Dr. Brown.

Jake scratched at his chin as his mind drifted. A shifter he rescued weeks ago overheard something between two scientists suggesting that their augmentations and experiments were tied to an attempt to open some sort of a portal. Jake wondered if some of the new abilities were supposed to be the key to open this fictional doorway.

A smile spread across his face as he realized that questioning Paige would be the logical next step. After all, if he needed more details about the machine—and Paige had been inside of it—then a witness was the best place to start.

"Earth to Paige," Ellie said as she picked up a French fry off her lunch tray and threw it. Paige jumped as the fry bounced off her forehead.

"Sorry. I guess my mind drifted." For a moment, she was back in the lab, being dragged down a dank hallway.

Ellie's face darkened. "Are you okay?" Her voice was soft and sincere amid the din of the cafeteria.

Paige looked around, rubbing her arm absently. "Yeah," she said with a shaky voice. Something had triggered the memory, but Paige couldn't identify anything nearby that would have triggered the thoughts—or flashbacks. "I was just thinking of the lab." Paige picked up a fry and took a small nibble. The oily taste churned her stomach. She put it back on the tray and tried to fake a smile at Ellie.

"It gets better. I promise," Ellie said sympathetically.

A familiar voice asked, "What gets better?"

Paige spun around to find Jake standing behind her. Butterflies swarmed in her belly, but instead of enjoying the sensation, Paige felt like she might be sick. The last thing she wanted was for Jake to witnessonce again—her at a most vulnerable moment. She was sick of feeling lost and scared. Sometimes she wasn't sure who she was. It was as if she suddenly realized that she was a tiger with spots instead of stripes. Despite all the people around her, Paige didn't know how to really let others in, leaving her feeling confused and alone.

"Did I drop by at a bad time?" Jake asked, the wide

smile fading from his face and his brown eyes softening, seeming to fill with worry.

"No," Paige said flatly. Anger prickled beneath her skin. She liked that emotion. It was familiar and comfortable somehow. Much better than the vulnerability.

Jake cleared his throat and fidgeted with the button on his blazer. "I just had some follow-up questions if you didn't mind..."

Paige sighed. In addition to rescuing her, Jake had been nothing but nice, and it was his job to investigate. She couldn't fault him for showing up when he needed more information.

"I'm done eating anyway," she said, grabbing the tray of half-eaten food. She dumped it into the garbage on her way out of the cafeteria after saying their goodbyes to Ellie. "Where to?" she asked Jake, peering back at him.

"We might find some privacy in the courtyard," Jake suggested.

Paige extended her arm as if to say, *Lead the way.* The courtyard hadn't been a place she had stopped yet while on her tour with Ellie. They'd only made it through the first floor of WANC before Paige's stomach rumbled at the smell of food in the cafeteria. So, they stopped to eat, planning to finish the tour of the facilities later. Paige had to admit that, so far, she had a lot more freedom than at the lab, even if she still felt confined at times.

She followed Jake into the courtyard, where gardens flanked the green patch of grass at its core. In the cooling fall weather, a few stubborn flowers still held their blooms, but most of them were dying or well on their way for hibernation before the winter. A few trees were filled with fiery leaves, but most already had bare branches. The smell of dry leaves flooded her senses, calming her. She smiled, remembering how much she loved this time of year—and feeling happy to remember *anything* about herself. Paige's favorite season, autumn, was coming to a close, but the temperature stayed mild in British Columbia, and the cold chill of winter could not be detected in the gentle breeze that played in her untamed hair.

Paige spotted a carved stone bench at the edge of the garden and perched on it. Jake's warm body flanked her. It was a perfect setup: the garden, the presence of someone who stirred something inside of her while also offering a much-needed comfort. She wanted to curl up in his arms and hide from the rest of the world. But that was too much to actually consider when there were so many unknowns in her life.

"How long have you been doing this for?" she wondered aloud.

"Doing what?"

"Rescuing shifters in distress." She peered up at him from under her eyelashes, batting them playfully. Paige picked at a patch of moss on the edge of the stone. It was all she could do to keep her mind off of undressing the hot FUC agent next to her. Her tiger wanted to pounce.

"Five years. But I don't think of it like that. You're all survivors."

Paige didn't feel like one. She felt like anything but. It was more like being a ghost of yourself. "So, you see a lot of…survivors." The word felt clunky on her tongue.

"I do. And for how difficult it can be, it is good work. Rewarding work. I feel like I am making a difference."

Paige raised a brow at him, cocking her head to the side. To her, it seemed like for every two steps forward, FUC took three back. She heard the stories of labs popping up faster than being discovered.

"Let me explain it this way," Jake started. "This story was told to me by my old FUC partner. There once was a little man in a boat—"

Paige interrupted with bouts of laughter. "A what?"

Jake smiled. "A little man in a boat."

"Okay." Paige tried to swallow her chuckles.

"He's lost at sea, no paddles, no food or water. He just has his boat." He cupped his hands for emphasis. "He thinks about giving up and just jumping overboard but soon realizes the ocean is full of other boats."

"So he flags down help?" Paige asked, unsure of what the point of the story was.

"Exactly. Survivors fight to the end. And to survive, sometimes you need to accept the help from others.

That doesn't make you any less of a survivor." He looked at her with such intensity her whole body warmed.

Who was she to argue when a man like that made such a persuasive argument?

"So, when you feel lost..." he prompted.

"I'll think of the little man in the boat." She smiled then rolled her eyes at how silly it sounded. Changing the subject, she asked, "Was there something you wanted to ask me?"

His deep brown eyes studied her for a moment as if trying to memorize her features. Jake squinted, seemingly struggling to find the right words before finally saying, "This might be difficult for you to talk about," he finally said.

His voice acted like a soft kiss on her senses, and Paige's mind wandered. She found herself wondering what it would be like if he leaned in closer, his breath in her ear, before trailing kisses down her neck. Her face flushed. Paige turned away so he wouldn't notice. "What do you want to ask?" she asked.

"We couldn't find the machine you described. Do you know if they took you off-site?"

Paige set her face in her hands and leaned forward. "I'm all right," she explained before he could ask. "I'm just trying to remember."

Closing her eyes, she let her mind drift back to the terrifying place where she was held captive. Though she knew she was physically safe, her body still reacted as if she were back there. Her pulse quickened, and her breathing became shallow as she focused on the moment before they took her from her cell. "They would inject me with something that made it difficult to move. Then they would put a sack over my head." A shiver crept up her spine as a loon cried nearby, as though echoing the one she heard back when she was running through the cornfield.

Jake wrapped his fingers around her hand. His skin warm and comforting. "Just remember you are safe now."

Page nodded as a tear streaked down her cheek. Her heart pounded so hard she wondered if it could break her ribs. Instead, she grounded herself, focusing on the feel of Jake's hand on hers. She pressed on through the memory. "They wheeled my bed down the hall and eventually picked me up and… yeah! They put me in a vehicle, I'm pretty sure! I remember the surface I laid on was cold and hard. Maybe it was the back of a cargo van?"

"You're doing great, Paige." Jake rubbed her back, doing whatever he could to keep her relaxed. He knew his request was difficult—asking her to relive her nightmare—but if there were more people in danger at a different facility, they needed to know. He would track the people who did this to Paige to the ends of the earth.

Paige lifted her head but kept her eyes closed. "I felt the movement. The vibration of the vehicle. Yes. If I had to go guess, I'd say, ten minutes? Hard to say for sure with all the drugs and such in my system, and the first ride felt like it took forever. Once we stopped, they would pull me out and carry me a short distance. I think we went into an elevator, and then it was a short distance from there to the machine. That's when they would take my hood off—after setting me inside." Paige's face looked somber as she slowly opened her eyes.

"You did great. That really helps," he assured her.

Her emerald eyes focused on his. "Do you think you can find the machine?"

Jake wanted to promise her the world. He wanted nothing more than to tell her this would never happen to anyone ever again. Instead, he said, "I hope so." His voice caught in his throat.

"What happened to the scientist in the field?" Her eyes were so full of hope. Jake wished that he could tell her that he was apprehended.

"You were my priority at the time. After I made sure that you were okay, I turned to find a pile of clothes. He must have shifted."

Paige's hopeful face dropped as if in defeat. Jake squeezed her hand. "Paige." She looked up at him, and her soft lips parted slightly. Jake wanted nothing more than to scoop her into his arms and kiss her pain away. He hungered for her. Her strength and stubbornness were sexy, but Jake could sense her softer side, too. He wanted to know everything about her. And that fiery look in her emerald eyes was intoxicating. But it wasn't time for that. The people behind the machine would not stop, and he had to keep his focus. "I will do whatever it takes to make sure we arrest everyone who was involved with this."

She put her soft hands on the side of his face and turned him to face her. The way she gazed into his eyes penetrated his soul. Were her feelings for him just as deep as his were for her? Jake feared he was letting his imagination get the best of him, but then, to his surprise, Paige leaned in and pressed her lips to his cheek, gifting him with an innocent kiss that ignited the primal side of him. Fire erupted in his chest and spread throughout his body. Jake attempted to quiet his fox side, which demanded he not pass up the chance to draw her into his arms and claim her right then and there.

"Thank you," she said with passion burning behind her eyes, though her voice was hardly audible, even for his shifter hearing. Then, before Jake could gather his wits, Paige stood and walked away without looking back.

Jake smiled. The hunt was on. He had to outfox some bad guys.

6

"Wait a minute," Ellie squealed after throwing her pillow at Paige from her bed. "You pecked him on the cheek and then got up and left?"

Paige nodded.

"What is wrong with you?" Ellie giggled.

"He's busy," Paige said flatly.

"I think Tall-Dark-and-Handsome would have made the time today to make out with you." She smiled mischievously, the setting sunlight through the window dancing in her eyes.

Paige looked to the floor, biting her lip. "What if he doesn't like me…like that?"

Ellie smiled widely. "Agent Park may look all business in his fancy suit, but whenever he's around you, his eyes eat you up."

"Sure, okay. So, what? We're supposed to go on a date in the cafeteria?" Paige threw her head back and laughed darkly. Despite the growing attraction she had for Agent Park—Jake—which she could no longer deny, the thought of trying to date while at the Academy was ridiculous. If only she could leave the Academy and go home. Start to feel like herself again. Then maybe she'd be more comfortable with the idea of a romance with Jake.

Except, she didn't know where her home was or if she'd ever know who she used to be. Paige let out a huge sigh of frustration as she leaned back against the wall next to her bed.

"No, silly!" Paige was sure that if Ellie had another pillow, she would have thrown it at her. "Go into town with Jake. It's super tiny, but there's a coffee shop, a diner, a little boutique, and even a pub. Oh, and a *motel.*" Ellie waggled her eyebrows at the last word.

Paige shook her head. *That* idea was far more ludicrous than dating in the cafeteria. "You think they're just going to let me leave?"

"No. They're going to let you go for dinner in the town with a sexy FUC agent as your chaperone." Ellie carefully enunciated her words for effect. She sat back against the wall, satisfied she won the argument.

She mulled the idea over in her mind—the dinner part, not the *motel* part. It would be nice to leave the sterile campus for a bit. Maybe sitting in a pub would let her mind reacclimate to a "normal" setting and allow some memories to come back. Plus... some alone time with Jake? She couldn't deny that sounded nice.

"Fine. I will ask for permission just so I can inform you that they told me no," she said defiantly, certain the doctors or the powers that be would let her leave the facility to go on a date.

"Good!" Ellie said, catching the pillow Paige threw back at her.

Then a thought occurred to her, and Paige looked down at her sweatsuit. The baggy clothes hung off of her tiny frame in the frumpiest of ways. She was certain that while she couldn't remember her life, she must have had more curves before starvation at the lab. That was one more thing to add to her list of things wrong with her—no memories, a strange shrieking ability, and a body that felt like a stranger's.

Paige's eyes began to burn as they filled with tears.

"What's wrong?" Ellie asked.

"What would I even wear?"

Ellie moved to her side. Immediately her new friend's arms were around Paige as she spilled hot tears onto her shoulder. "The FUC-issued sweatsuit isn't your only option! There are clothing donations we have access to. It's like our own little thrift store. And if they don't have anything decent, like a pair of jeans and a pretty shirt, we can ask around and see if anyone has something they're willing to loan. I guarantee you that they will. You worry about getting the permission to go, and I will find you something to wear."

Paige felt the loose threads that held her together were fraying, threatening to let her come undone. She couldn't remember much of her past, yet she was planning to ask a man out. "What if I am moving too fast? Shouldn't I be in intensive therapy instead of dating?"

"Nonsense!" Ellie chuckled. "I mean, do the therapy thing too, but sometimes doing something normal is exactly what we need." She squeezed Paige's arm.

Paige sniffled, contemplating her options. She felt so safe every time she was around Jake. Even her urges to let her anger act as a shield had lessened when he was near. But it seemed too much to hope that it was true, that there could be something between them. "What if he says no?"

"If he says no, I'll beam him up to the Arctic to think about his mistake."

"You can do that?" Paige's eyes widened at the thought.

Ellie scrunched up her face in contemplation. "No, but if I could, I would, for you."

"Thanks." Paige's heart swelled at Ellie's loyalty. Even though they'd just met, Paige felt like she'd known her forever. And maybe she did, in some buried recollection. "If you need anyone mauled by a tiger, you let me know," Paige joked.

The next day was filled with doctor's appointments. As Dr. Brown had assured her, she was given the option to opt-out of tests, but she went along with everything asked of her. Partly because she wanted to find out what had been done to her and also partly because she wanted to show she was cooperative so she could receive permission to go into town with Jake.

To her irritation, none of the doctors, nurses, or lab techs that she came into contact with would speak to if she was allowed to leave the premises. Many of them told her—in a nice way that somehow still felt punitive—that it was too soon to speak in regards to her stability and healing. One of them mused that being accompanied by an agent would probably be the only way she could leave the premises at this time but also said that she couldn't commit to a response at this time. One of them mentioned that she would start therapy soon and could ask her counselor. It left Paige trying not to huff in frustration over the lack of straight answers. It was disappointing, to say the least.

Before heading back to her room after her last round of bloodwork, Paige decided to indulge herself by re-visiting the bench where she'd kissed Jake. She weaved through the well-trimmed grass in the yard, noting as she grew closer that the soft scent of his cologne lingered—or was it just her memory of it?—mingling with that of the damp stone of the bench. It tickled her nostrils and tightened her loins. The more frustrated she grew with the lack of answers from her doctors, the stronger her passion for Jake grew. *Blame it on my rebellious side,* she thought. Though maybe that was just an excuse to let her true feelings flow freely inside of her. Jake balanced her, bringing her feelings into harmony. When he was around, she had hope, serenity, and all those other positive feelings she feared had died from her time in the lab. Paige felt at home around him.

Her hand explored the rough marble of the bench as she longed for Jake to be sitting next to her again. A pang twinged in her chest as she wondered when she would see him again. Though she'd yet to confirm it with him, she felt pretty sure that Jake had feelings for her. Why else would he personally escort her to her dorm or question her about the lab? He could have easily let someone else do it.

Without warning, a shiver crept up her spine, making the hair on her neck stand up, one by one. She was being watched. The feeling unsettled her, and she let go of her thoughts of Jake as she glanced around, unable to shake the sensation. A few cadets chatted a ways away, but they clearly were interested in their conversation and paying Paige no mind. She spotted two red squirrels scrambling around a nearby tree and a lone loon—a duck-like bird with a black face, white chest, and grey body—pecking at grubs on the far side of the courtyard. No other creatures could be seen.

Paige remained uneasy. *What if those squirrels are shifters?* She wondered as paranoia set in. *Or the loon? Why is it so far from water?* Suddenly, it seemed as if the trees had eyes and were spying on her. A tightness spread across her chest as she struggled to breathe. She shot up off the bench and ran toward WANC. Her feet stomped on the hard ground, feeling heavier and heavier as the glass door seemed to stretch farther away with each step. Her panic told her she was running for her life from an invisible enemy she couldn't see but knew was there.

Her breaths screeched in noisily as she fought against hyperventilating. She tried to keep them slow and even, but Paige felt strangled. After finally reaching the door, Paige ripped it open and tumbled inside, her knees instantly giving out. She curled up on the cool floor, sobbing into her hands.

"Paige!" Ellie squealed from down the hall. Instantly, her friend was at her side, her warm arms around her. "What happened?"

"I-I don't know." It was difficult to talk. Paige was still trying to catch her breath.

"Oh my God. You're shaking." Fear laced Ellie's voice. "Let me take you to the doc—"

"No," Paige said, more forcefully than she intended. "I just…felt confined."

"Confined. Outside?" Ellie's voice was soft and calming, but her face looked confused.

"I…" Paige glanced around the hall at the other shifters, who pretended she wasn't sitting on the floor crying. She struggled to find the right words, swallowing hard as she tried to replay the events in her mind. "I felt like I was being watched. And when I couldn't see anyone, I was afraid all the animals outside were shifter scientists from other labs." The words spilled out of her, tumbling out. She felt relief once she admitted what she suspected. It sounded crazy, but at least she had someone to talk to.

Ellie squeezed her tightly. "I don't know if this is the right thing to say, but you might have PTSD or something."

Paige sniffed as the people in the halls continued to flow around them like a school of salmon navigating a stream around obstacles. "Actually, since I was rescued a couple of days ago, it would be acute stress disorder. Post-traumatic stress disorder can only be diagnosed if the symptoms occur a month or so after the trauma."

"Oh," Ellie replied, her eyes wide. "I didn't know that."

"I didn't *know* I knew that... *How* do I know that?" Paige asked, leaning back against the wall as her breathing began to even out while, slowly and steady, her mind began to clear. She somehow knew about mental disorders. The puzzle that was her life started coming together, a small piece at a time.

"I have no idea." Ellie shook her head. "When is your first appointment with your therapist? You should probably discuss it with them."

"Tomorrow, I think," Paige replied, processing the newly acquired old knowledge as just another layer of foggy memories to add to the mix. She couldn't identify how she knew it, just that she just did, just like the brief moments from her early childhood that would flash in her mind from time to time. Aside from that, she felt like a boat adrift at sea. It was disorienting. Paige didn't think she could discern the best way forward without knowing her past.

Could she? Paige thought about Jake. He made her feel like the future held possibilities, whether or not she knew where she came from. He was understanding when she was frustrated and angry. He projected a sense of calmness that made her feel like home could be made anew.

"Are you thinking of Jake again?" Ellie asked, a wide smile spreading across her face.

Paige's shoulders bounced as she bashfully nodded. "How could you tell?" She began to peel herself up off of the floor with the help of Ellie.

"You always look… happy when you think of him."

Paige returned the grin. It was difficult for her to accept help at times, but Jake had been there when she most needed it over the last few days and was able to cut through her bullshit and comfort her, like a sunny day calming rough seas. He hadn't treated her with special kid gloves or anything, either. She believed he was accepting of her, just the way she was, traumatized and seemingly broken. If Jake didn't see her as a defective person, did that mean maybe she wasn't?

She hoped her reading of Jake's actions weren't off base. Could she trust her woman's intuition? Because she felt drawn to him, wanted to get to know him more, wanted to lay eyes on him and have more time to appreciate how well he filled out that suit, like a movie star in a cop drama.

Jake was sexy as hell. There was no more trying to deny that.

Paige only hoped that she would be able to see him again soon. This tigress was ready to pounce.

7

A chilly breeze ushered in the indigo sky of the night as Jake wrapped up his meeting with a contact at the nearest hydro station. He was operating on the theory that the machine Paige described would need a lot of power, but so far, he couldn't pinpoint any particular strains on the grid. Jake had hit a dead end. He rubbed at the stubble forming on his jaw. Chasing down these scientists was starting to feel like cockroach eradication. Just when you tracked one down, three more scurried in opposite directions. How would they ever be able to track them all down and make them accountable for the inhumane experiments they were conducting? He sighed. One at a time, little by little. The good guys had to be persistent, and someday they might be able to trap them all.

At the very least, he had to focus on the fact that

they were helping people. Freeing them from cages and helping them to learn to live again.

Like Paige.

Jake sighed again as he climbed into his SUV. He'd hoped to tell Paige that he arrested the people who did this to her. When he couldn't locate the bad guy, Jake took it personally. It haunted him just as his mother's screams echoed in his memory. He was never that far away from being that worried kid in his room, feeling alone and helpless while others suffered with nightmares. It wasn't a good place to be.

Growing up and seeing the fear his mother had, knowing the scientist who tortured her had not been caught, was intolerable. She looked over her shoulder, tense over being captured again for years. If the phone rang and the person on the other line didn't speak, she would break down in hysterics, afraid it was him. Jake didn't want the same thing happening to Paige. He wanted to right the wrongs of his past to give Paige a brighter future.

He twisted the key in the ignition, and the engine came to life, as did the radio, which thankfully drowned out the screams of his imagination. For the moment, anyway.

Jake eased the gear shift into Drive and pulled out of the parking spot. Rush hour traffic spilled down the main route like water from a burst dam. He merged with the flow of it, blending in with the others scrambling to get home after work. It was a long drive into the mountains to get to the secluded location of FUCN'A, but it was worth it for the chance to see Paige. He craved her presence.

Jake imagined the moment he caught the bad guys. He could see Paige rushing into his arms for a passionate kiss. But alas, that wouldn't happen anytime soon. But the case wasn't going as he conceptualized. He felt like a failure yet still wanted to see her again. He just hoped that she felt the same way.

Paige was abrasive at first, but Jake understood. Her life had been turned upside-down by the scientists who experimented on her. It was probably hard to know who to trust after an ordeal like that.

When he finally weaved through the parked cars at WANC, his mind raced with thoughts about what excuse he would give Paige for visiting again, especially when it was close to nine o'clock at night. As he entered the building, he still had no justification for coming back to see her. That last thing he wanted was to come off looking like a creeper—or a stalker. Jake's dress shoes padded down the hallway as autopilot took him to the dorms.

What's so wrong with the truth? He wondered as he strolled closer to Paige's room. Why couldn't he knock on her door and say, "Hey! I was having a shitty day, and you were the one person I wanted to see, so I thought I'd stop by." With each step closer to her, Jake felt his confidence fading. He hesitated at her doorway before knocking, still unsure how to proceed. *Gotta rip it off like a Band-Aid,* he thought as he raised his hand—just as Paige jerked open the door from the other side. Jake practically rapped his knuckles on her forehead.

He stared at her with his mouth open, his mind completely blank. Why did things never go as expected when he was around her? She propped her hands on her hips, cocking her head sideways, her black hair cascading down as she took him in with her green eyes sweeping every inch of him.

"Ellie!" Paige called over her shoulder, breaking the excruciating silence. "Did you order a stripper for me?"

"Stripper? What?" Jake blurted out, finally free of his stupor.

Ellie sauntered over, the shadows rippling off her body with the motion. "Agent Park. Do you have a side hustle?" She winked at him.

"*I'mnotastripper*!" he shouted as if it were one word.

Paige giggled, his awkwardness seemingly feeding her sense of humor. "What brings you here at such a late hour then?"

He puffed up his chest and rolled his shoulders back. "An agent of FUC is never off duty," he said in the most official voice he could muster.

Paige's form deflated with a sigh. "I am not in the mood for any more questions tonight." She shook her head with what Jake read as disappointment and moved to shut the door.

Jake held up a hand to stop her. "I'm not here for questioning."

"Not a stripper and not here for FUC..." Ellie mumbled, walking out of his view back into the depths of the dorm room.

"What are you here for then, Agent Park?" Paige asked, chewing her lip and over-enunciating his name in a way that warmed his loins. No woman's voice had ever had that effect on him before. Jake's heart quickened.

"I had a bad day and wanted to see you again." Jake decided to go for it—to try being direct and honest. He wanted—no, needed—Paige to know his affection for her. He feared she did not share his feelings but decided the risk was worth it. This wasn't an everyday occurrence for him, and he couldn't let the chance of there being something real between them slip away. The earlier kiss from the garden lingered on his cheek, a searing memory that refused to let him forget about how much more he wanted.

"My day sucked too..." she replied, her green eyes looking off to the side and becoming unfocused.

"I didn't mean..." Jake fumbled with his words. That last thing he wanted to do was to insinuate that his day was in any way comparable to that of someone who had just been freed from a bunch of mad scientists. "I just..."

"You don't have to tiptoe around me. You're allowed to have a bad day." Paige placed a firm hand on his bicep, and she smiled warmly. It lit up her face, reaching all the way to her eyes. "Do you want to go for a walk? "

"That sounds like a great idea." He beamed at her.

A joy that mirrored his warmed her face. "I just need to grab my sweatshirt." Paige disappeared from view for a moment before reemerging as she eased into a long-sleeved sweatshirt and then smoothed out her hair. It took all of Jake's willpower to not run his fingers through her silky tresses.

"Ready?" he asked, moving aside for her to step into the hallway.

She nodded. "Where to? I mean, I know I suggested the walk, but I don't really know where a walking path might be."

Jake bit his lip, trying to keep his mind focused, but it kept going back to how beautiful Paige looked, illuminated by the soft glow of the fluorescent lights of the hall. "I think the obstacle course would be free this time of night."

"Obstacle course?" Paige asked after waving a quick goodbye to Ellie as the door to their room shut with a click. She raised an eyebrow in confusion.

"I mean, not that we would have to *do* the obstacle course, but we can stroll on the track around it."

"Can we shift?" Paige's voice was soft, timid almost.

He raised an eyebrow, surprised. "Yeah, I didn't even think of that. The Academy has tons of land for shifters to run on." Jake's heart began to race. As much as he'd looked forward to talking with her, there was almost something more intimate about being in their other forms together. Moving into your animal shape let you forget all the drama of the human world as you ran across the earth on four paws.

Not to mention, he'd be in close proximity to a naked Paige. Not for long, as they'd quickly change into their animal forms, but they would still be unclothed together. Jake planned on being the perfect gentleman—by not sneaking any peeks—but his body responded all the same. He wondered if she could sense his arousal. Heat filled his cheeks as he blushed at the thought.

The full moon basked the buildings and neatly manicured grass in a silver glow as they stepped outside. Paige reflected on how romantic it all was—even if she was wearing sweatpants. She still could not believe that Jake had shown up at her door. It was exactly what she was hoping for.

The way he acted around her had a sweet, almost bumbling awkwardness to it. As though the moment he got around her, he forgot all his composure. It was a huge contrast to the fierce man she first glimpsed in the cornfield—the one who'd swiftly and gracefully tangled with and taken down the scientist with the taser. A man like that was not to be messed with, yet he approached her with a genuineness laced with gentleness. Understanding she could affect such a powerful man in that way turned her on. Actually, just Jake in a suit turned her on. Paige wasn't sure if men of her past relationships dressed similarly, or maybe it was the authority that Jake represented that excited her.

Her desires lit a fire in her core. It tingled and spread throughout her torso, warm enough to keep the chill of the night air from stinging her flesh. She could practically feel the heat of Jake's body as he strolled next to her. Paige wanted to press against him, taking in every sensation that was Jake Park.

"D-do you want to shift?" Jake turned to her, interrupting her thoughts as they approached the tree line. A blush crept up his cheeks as she looked over Paige's shoulder instead of making eye contact, an act of shyness she didn't know he possessed.

Paige reached out with her fingertips, pressing his chin gently yet firm until he had locked eyes on her again. His brown eyes seemed to drink the light of the moon. Paige was intoxicated by every aspect of him. "I would love to." She refrained from adding, "I can't wait to see your firm, toned body," but she figured that would be too forward. Nakedness was a natural part of life for most shifters, especially those that morphed into larger creatures. If you didn't want to ruin your clothes—or risk them getting stuck on and looking utterly ridiculous—you removed them prior to the change.

Jake's shoulders eased as the tension left his body.

Paige lowered her hand, reaching for the lapel of Jake's suit jacket. She was mindful of his reaction, and when Jake didn't flinch, she raised her other hand to peel back the outer layer of clothing. His eyes narrowed, watching her with a passionate intensity that penetrated to her core. Paige's being smoldered with lust, but she fought to temper it for fear of coming on too strong.

The covering fell in the damp grass at his feet. Jake's breathing was even and deep. Paige wanted desperately for their lips to meet. She ached for his tongue to probe her mouth, but that was for another time. Now, she was satisfied at the thought of her hands roaming over his perfect form as she undressed him.

Paige's heart fluttered as her apt fingertips roamed across his firm chest toward the buttons of his dress shirt. The faint scent of lavender danced off of his garment as her palms traversed the soft fabric. She popped open the closures one at a time. His bare chest slowly emerged as the edges of the garment parted. Jake closed his eyes as her hands glided across his taut muscles. Soon Jake's torso was free of his shirt. Paige's eyes skimmed over every delicious inch of him, devouring the image.

The soft moonlight rippled across his washboard abs as if they were flowing rapids of a stream. After drinking in his image with her eyes, Paige wanted to explore his body with her fingers. When she slid her palms down to this belt, he put a gentle hand on hers. "I can manage the rest. You need to catch up." He winked at her.

Paige undressed fast, leaving her clothes in a pile at her now bare feet. The cold blades of grass slipped between her toes as she turned to face Jake. She crossed her arms, hoping to hide the ripple of ribs beneath her skin. The act was in vain, as Jake was the perfect gentleman. His eyes never wavered off her face.

"Your eyes are beautiful," he finally said. Jake's voice was honey in her ears.

She felt the corners of her mouth turn up as a slow smile spread across her face, melting away her insecurities. The people of the lab may have sought to destroy her, to take her humanity, but they could never penetrate her deep enough to do so. And all the experimentation in the world couldn't numb her to this moment with Jake. If she had to endure the torture all over again just for the chance to meet him, she would. The new memory she was forming right now was worth the price she had paid.

A shiver jolted her shoulders as the night breeze tickled her bare skin. "Let's shift before you freeze," Jake commanded, soft yet firm, his protector side coming out.

Paige nodded, trying to keep her eyes from wandering across his yummy frame. She had yearned for the chance to let her Siberian tiger emerge. The scientists at the lab had suppressed it for too long.

Shifting was a dance etched in her mind, a natural

rhythm that flowed through her limbs. Paige let her tiger free. As it pranced to the surface, she pressed her palms into the damp grass. Her legs shortened and mutated with a familiar feeling. The change rippled through her body, transforming bones and stretching ligaments. Fur sprouted across her skin, rippling across her in a tingling sensation.

The colors of the world muted as her feline eyes took it in. Her peripheral vision sharpened, bringing more of the surrounding obstacle course into focus. She could feel every individual blade of grass as it was matted beneath her sensitive pads as she sauntered toward the new Jake. He curved his red, bushy fox tail around his feet as her massive form neared him.

Jake swiveled his head, his pointed snout directing Paige's attention to the forest. In a swift motion, he sprang up off of his haunches and slid off into the night. Paige padded along behind him, trying her best to keep her pace with his. Stretching her tiger legs felt amazing. It had been trapped inside for far too long. The world had so many scents and sounds that she missed when taking the form of a person. It was true that her senses were sharper than a regular human, but her surroundings were saturated with information as an animal. She scented the multitude of other shifters who ran the path earlier. The grass felt softer where their feet had landed hours before. All this was easily overlooked by non-animal perceptions. It was as if the world was back in three dimensions after being trapped in only two. If big cats could purr, she would.

Jake's tail swished in a rhythm with his pace. Her feline eyes were drawn to the motion, like a housecat to a dangling string. As he quickened the pace, she trotted along, feeling the breeze tousling her fur. The feeling of freedom sank into her bones. After her captivity, this tigress was finally free to roam. It was intoxicating.

A towering pine caught her attention. She bounded toward it, launching herself into its sticky branches. Her claws dug for purchase before she settled on one of the broad bows that could hold her weight. The musky scent reminded her of the holidays and her father. Many good memories were tangled into that smell, even if the sap would cling to her for days.

Jake's fox maneuvered up the tree, perching on one of the lower branches to Paige's amazement. She didn't know foxes could climb. As if reading her mind, Jake began scurrying farther up the tree. Soon she couldn't see him. All she could hear was the scratching of his claws. Then suddenly he slid past her, gliding as the branches flattened below him. He gracefully landed on the ground as if he'd done this a thousand times before. He hopped around, wagging his bushy tail playfully, gesturing for Paige to try it out.

She glanced up at the branches nervously. The higher ones may have held the weight of a fox, but she wasn't about to find out how they'd fare against a feline her size. *Nope, not today, not on my first time back in my fur!*

Instead, she leaped from her branch to the ground in a fluid motion. *Let him call me a scaredy-cat,* she thought. It was more important to enjoy the freedom than to try to prove something and end up laid up in the hospital wing again.

He seemed to bark a chuckle at her, seemingly taunting her. She bared her teeth with a playful growl in return before frolicking off through the row of trees. The fox chased after her but couldn't keep her pace. Finally, she slowed and plopped down to rest beneath a tree, curling up as if to show how long she was waiting for him. After a brief moment, Jake's fox appeared, panting and looking a bit winded.

He nodded his head over his shoulder, beckoning her to follow him back out of the woods. Paige didn't want the feeling to end but knew she needed rest. Her body was still recovering after being captive and starved for so long. She didn't want to push it. She padded softly behind the tiny fox, her eyes fixed on his swishing tail. He was truly graceful and beautiful in animal form.

Jake's steps slowed as he led them back to the pile of clothes peeled off earlier. Her paws wanted to continue investigating the campus, but she knew he was right as he sat next to his clothing, refusing to complete another loop. It was getting late. The moon had already started its descent past the zenith.

The chill of the night felt more severe, cutting into her human skin as she morphed out of her tiger fur. Paige quickly threw her clothes back on, her teeth chattering. Jake sauntered over, already dressed and placing his blazer across her shoulders.

"Would you go to dinner with me?" The words were out of her mouth, tumbling over her lips in an avalanche before she knew it.

Jake's forehead creased as his eyebrows raised. "Are your doctors all right with that idea? I mean, you're not a prisoner here, but I want you to be safe."

Paige bit her lip. She had tried convincing them all day without any headway. "Maybe if you talk to them, they would realize that *you* would keep me protected."

Her heart fluttered as Jake replied, "It doesn't hurt to ask."

8

Paige found Ellie back in their room, all a flutter at the possibility of her going on a date off-campus with Jake. "So, I know you could check out the donations or borrow some clothing, but I found out there's this thing called NAKED—the Network for Apparel and Kit Express Delivery. They shop for you and drop it right off where you need it. This way, you could get some new stuff that you choose, and it would be fun to pick out an outfit for your date..."

"I don't have any money," Paige replied.

Ellie flashed a plastic card. "You're in luck! There's a FUC agent here, Kailee Goosby-Watkins, who's like super-rich or something and also happens to highly believe in retail therapy. I heard from one of the other experiments that I should go tell her what was going on with you, and she was happy to help!"

"She gave you a gift card for online shopping?"

"Yep!" Ellie beamed.

"I don't know if the doctors will give it their blessing." Paige hesitated, not wanting her hopes to be too high in the event that they did not give their permission. She didn't want to add crushed to her list of current unwanted emotions, especially after so many were randomly cropping up.

"Oh, don't be such a stick in the mud! What else are you going to do today?" Ellie tossed a pillow her way. Paige punched it away before it whacked her face.

She had to admit her roommate had a point. Picking out a cute NAKED outfit was probably more enjoyable than anything else they had going on. Paige had been informed by one of the staff that she would meet her counselor, Edith Daya, later. Aside from using the session to obtain permission for her date, Paige was not interested in therapy. Having something to distract her from the impending session and help pass the time would be welcome. "Oh, okay. Let's go online shopping!" A grin spread across Paige's face as the tension melted from her shoulders. Maybe she needed more fun in her life than she realized.

"Yes!" Ellie squealed, scrunching her eyes tight in excitement as she hopped off her bed. Even her shadows appeared delighted as they flowed off of her in smooth swirls. She sailed across the tiny room, grabbing Paige by the wrist. "To the library!" she proclaimed, pointing forward with her free hand.

"Are you living vicariously through me?" Paige

asked as they entered the hall. Two staff members chatted as they passed the duo, clutching their morning coffees.

"Hmm..." Ellis cocked her head to the side. "Maybe."

Paige felt she could not have had a better roommate if she had picked one out herself. Ellie's bubbly demeanor helped to raise Paige's spirits and give her hope for the future. The temptation was so strong at times to mope in their room, but Ellie kept Paige talking. After every conversation, it was as if a weight had been removed. It was true that Ellie had been rescued mere weeks before Paige, but she suspected that Ellie had some natural way of not falling to pieces from the trauma. She just seemed more resilient, stronger somehow than Paige felt. Paige was more abrasive, prickly even. But Ellie pushed through her hard exterior and supported her every step of the way.

Just like Jake did.

They weaved through hallways and traveled briefly down a floor in the elevator. Paige was amazed at how well Ellie knew the building. Paige could hardly remember how to find the cafeteria.

Ellie recounted how she came across the library by mistake one day. She admitted to visiting it frequently when she felt lonely. "Most of the books are related to the subjects they teach at the Academy, but even *that* is eye-opening if you weren't a shifter before." She turned back and smiled at Paige, but it didn't quite reach her eyes. Paige wondered if there was more to her than met the eye. "I thought my head would explode my first week here, but I am getting used to things now," she added with a shrug. Paige was about to ask how Ellie had been adjusting to suddenly being a shifter when Ellie changed the subject, "The library should be pretty dead this time of day. Most of the cadets are in class."

Two double doors appeared as they turned the next corner. "WANC Library" was inscribed in a brass plaque above them. Ellie swung open the door, and Paige was greeted by shelves filled with wide-spined reference volumes and a row of unoccupied computers. The dusty smell of dried paper and the hum of electricity welcomed them. Something normal was a feast for her senses, awakening a feeling of safety within Paige.

Ellie took a seat at the nearest computer, and Paige rolled a chair next to her. Ellie's apt fingers flew across the keys as she explained to Paige how they could log in as a guest and use the internet. "Though it's heavily firewalled and limited. FUC doesn't want us going around posting information we shouldn't or learning about anything that might harm our delicate psyches."

"Sure, makes sense."

Ellie pulled up the NAKED site. "There's nothing too fancy in town, so I am guessing we should stay away from the 'formal' category," Ellie noted, moving the mouse across the categories of clothing offered.

Paige's eyes roamed the page. "I am not sure what

my style was." The realization brought disappointment with it. Paige had hoped that perusing clothing would help her to remember something about who she'd been.

Ellie placed a sympathetic hand on her arm. "Maybe the question shouldn't be who you were as much as, who do you want to be? Think of yourself as a blank slate. You can dress however you like. What do you envision wearing on a date with Agent Jake Park?"

Paige's chest rose as she inhaled deeply, closing her eyes to bring forth an image of herself. She let her mind fill in the blanks until she had a detailed concept of what felt like the correct attire for her to don. "Do they have baseball shirts? But female ones that fit tightly."

"They have everything." Ellie smiled. "It's not like we have to shop just from the tiny town boutique. They'll deliver from the city if needed!"

They found a shirt she liked, and she also picked out straight-leg jeans and canvas sneakers. Seeing the outfit all together pleased Paige. She was relieved to have something other than a sweatsuit to wear.

But she also worried. "Am I getting ahead of myself?" *What if he agreed to dinner only because he didn't know how to turn me down?* The thought was crushing. Maybe her asking him out threw him off and he couldn't say no at the time.

"Why would you ask that?" Ellie's brow furrowed, and her head cocked slightly to the side.

Paige sighed. A strand of hair fluttered in her breath. "Jake never actually asked me to dinner. He just went along with it when I asked him out."

Ellie raised an eyebrow at her, a smirk spreading across her face. "That man is *not* going along with anything!"

"How can you be sure?" Emotions were swirling inside Paige. Anxiety, guilt, worthlessness, emptiness, and hope. She wanted to be sure she wasn't just clinging to hope and living in a dream world.

"He has made so many *excuses* to see you. And think about it. How easy would it have been for him to say *no, I can't go with you because you don't have permission."* Ellie lowered her voice to a silly octave to mimic Jake. "Or even easier, he could have told you *it's unprofessional for me to see you outside of the Academy,* and that would have been the end of it. But he didn't. *Plus,* he *told* you yesterday that he *wanted* to see you. He's into you, Paige. Just accept it."

Paige couldn't argue the logic. "You have a point. Now I just gotta see if my counselor will approve me leaving campus for a date." The thought of asking permission from someone she had never met was daunting. But if she had to do it to feel a little normal—and to date a hottie—she would.

"Just be honest with her," Ellie coaxed. "I've met with Dr. Daya. She's pretty cool."

Paige didn't like the idea of talking about things she wanted to forget and not being able to discuss what she wanted to remember. Feeling like a stranger in her own life was getting old. But she supposed she needed to give this counseling thing a shot if it meant she had a chance to leave the campus to go on a date with Jake.

9

"Please. I'll be good." Paige smiled at her counselor. Their appointment was ending, yet Paige feared that she wouldn't be granted clearance to leave the grounds. Especially after admitting to the panic attack she had the other day.

Edith rubbed her chin and squinted as if inspecting Paige. "It's not that I don't *trust* you. It's just a matter of whether or not it's in your best interest and if there is a potential for harm to the general public. Having a panic attack at the pub would be potentially unsafe for you but even worse if the screaming incident repeated and harmed civilians. Not to mention, would it damage your mental health if you felt an episode would negatively affect your developing relationship with Agent Park?"

Paige scrunched up her brow. "I see your point, but I feel pretty confident that the scream only happened because I was being threatened, and the panic attack only happened because I was alone."

Edith picked up her pen and placed it between her teeth while studying her notes. "I have here several mentions of loons. The one you saw in the yard when you had the panic episode. The one you heard while sitting with Jake the day before that. And you also heard one when you escaped the facility. It might be a sort of trigger for you at the moment."

Paige snorted. This was the Freudian psychobabble she'd dreaded being subjected to. It was so ridiculous, but Paige suspected if she let her views of therapy be known, she would never see outside the FUCN'A walls. Paige felt it was great for everyone else but hated to be the one under the microscope. She hated the vulnerability that came with being the one sitting on the couch while someone analyzed her. "I don't think it's anything specific to a common Canadian water bird. I just became paranoid that I was being watched. That has never happened when I have gone outside with Jake. I feel *safe* with him." Her heart fluttered just thinking of their time together. A smile tugged at the corner of her lips.

Edith removed the pen from her mouth and tapped in on the arm of her chair, eyeing Paige as if she could see the inner workings of her mind. Finally, she gave a definitive nod. "Fine."

"Wait. What do you mean 'fine'?" Paige cocked her

head to the side, thinking that there must be some sort of a catch.

"I mean," Edith said, settling back into her chair and crossing her legs nonchalantly, "if you do not experience any more panic attacks this week, I will allow you to leave with Agent Park for three hours this Friday."

She clasped her hands together triumphantly. "Thank you!"

"You are not to leave his sight, and I am going to make sure Agent Park understands this as well," Edith stated before giving Paige instructions and other contingencies for her date.

Paige nodded as if listening, but her mind was a blur. Going into the counseling session, Paige thought it was a fool's errand, yet her wish had now been granted.

"Of course," Paige said, unsure of what she agreed to. For all she knew, she just agreed to Jake dressing up in a hula skirt. She sprang up out of the chair, excited to tell Ellie—and especially Jake—the good news.

Edith cleared her throat, stopping Paige in her tracks. "Aren't you forgetting something?" Paige pivoted to see a white card in Edith's hand. "You will need this to leave the premises."

A shy smile spread across Paige's face. "Of course," she said, pretending she had listened to everything her counselor had just said. After slipping the card into her pocket, Paige skipped out of the office.

Paige burst into their dorm room, eager to pass the

news on to Ellie. "I have her permission! She is letting me go out this Friday."

A squeal escaped Ellie's lips before she popped across the room, instantly at Paige's side, hugging her tightly. "I told you it would work out! Now we just have to wait for your NAKED order to arrive."

But Paige hardly heard her friend. Instead, her attention snapped to the loon perched right outside their window on the frame. It seemed to be staring directly at her, its beady eyes reflecting the sun in a way that made it look like they were glowing red.

Surely it was just a coincidence. And birds didn't stalk people…

Sounds of the room became muffled as Paige's blood pressure soared, her heart pumping hard, seemingly trying to crack her breastbone.

"Paige?" Ellie grabbed her arm and turned her away from the window. "What is wrong?"

Paige pointed a finger back to the window. "What is *that* doing there?" The loon leered at her through the glass with its head cocked sideways.

"Oh, that? I think it's lost or something. I've seen it hanging around there a few times lately." Ellie chewed on her fingernail. "Though this is the first time I've seen it on the sill, staring in here like that."

The loon continued to bore into the room with its red eyes. A gust of wind hit it, and it flapped its wings as it battled to keep its balance. Its webbed feet struggled to grip the shallow wooden ledge.

"Why doesn't it go back to the pond or the lake? Why is it fighting so hard to stay at our window?"

"I'm sure some blockheads broke the rules and fed it, so now it thinks if it hangs around, it will get more." Ellie's voice wavered in shaky syllables. Her words didn't sound confident. "Or maybe something scared it up here."

"Do you think it's a shifter?" Paige asked, wondering if it was the same loon from the garden. Was it possible that her instincts had been right? Perhaps she felt she was being watched that day in the garden because she *was*.

"There's no way for me or you to tell for sure. Maybe we can report it to someone."

"No!" Paige shouted louder than she meant to. "If it gets back to counselor Edith that I think a *loon* is stalking me, she'll never let me go to dinner with Jake."

Ellie sat on her bed. "It is rather odd that a loon is sitting on our windowsill. I understand why you wouldn't want to tell Dr. Daya, but I think we should at least tell Jake. You know...in case it is a shifter."

They both stared at the bird in silence until it squawked uncharacteristically and then pecked the window with a loud thud. Paige jumped at the sudden noise then reacted instantly, rapping the window with the palm-side of her fist. She made an impact with the glass right at level with the bird's head, startling it and causing it to fluff its wings and fly away.

Warm sunlight filtered through the pane, yet Paige

couldn't take her eyes off of the bird's perch. The only plausible explanation seemed to be that it was a shifter. Paige still didn't want to risk her counselor finding out and canceling her date.

But in her mind lingered the thought that someone was looking for her. Someone from the lab. Someone who could shift into a loon.

She tried to shake it off. The lab was cleared out and overrun with FUC agents. None of the scientists who might have escaped would be dumb enough to stay in the area, especially not to spy on one lone tiger shifter.

But was she really ready to risk it?

"I think you are right," Paige admitted. "Something is off about that bird, and Jake needs to hear about it."

10

"So…" Jake sipped his coffee, carefully listening to Paige's story about the loon. "It stood on the ledge of a third-story window and—"

"I know it sounds crazy, but I am certain it was spying on me."

Jake didn't like the concern in Paige's voice. After he surprised her by showing up at her dorm room with the best coffee in town, she asked if they could go to the library to talk in private. He worried she wanted to tell him that she didn't want to spend time with him anymore, so he was caught off-guard when Paige started describing a loon snooping around. He wrestled with a feeling of guilt that he'd put his duty as FUC agent to the side and was getting personal with someone he was supposed to protect. Had his feelings for her placed her in jeopardy?

"I will check the database for any loon shifters on

our persons-of-interest list. This could just be a mundane loon who's lost. Maybe it got in a fight over territory and hasn't found a new lake to call home yet, but I don't want to take any chances. I will check for connections to the lab where you were found, too." Jake wished he could have reassured her that this was nothing to worry about, but he was unable to. Something about the loon seemed familiar, and he wouldn't lie to her just to make her feel better. He would check the files and pictures of the lab again to confirm his suspicions. Paige deserved to know if there was someone possibly after her. And loons generally didn't hang out on windowsills.

"Just my luck," she spat out.

"What do you mean?"

"I actually got permission to go out with you this Friday, and then this stupid bird shows up." She sat on the nearest desk, her shoulders hunching forward in defeat.

Jake's heart ached at the sight. Paige had just been through an unspeakable atrocity, and all she wanted was to be able to go out for dinner and pretend that everything was normal for just one night.

He stepped toward her, pulling her into his arms. She laid her cheek on his shoulder, instantly melting into him. The rigidity of her muscles dissipated at his touch. He ran his hand over her hair, smoothing the silky strands with his fingers as he stroked them.

"I am going to make sure that you will be safe when

we go out, even if I have to request extra agents for your protection." He tilted her chin up at him with a finger. Light sparkled in her green eyes. Her full lips beckoned for his. Jake wanted to taste her, to feel her warm body. He had to resist... They were in a library, after all!

Paige eased up off the table from under Jake's intense gaze. His cologne danced in the air, musky and cool. It excited her, almost as much as being this close to him was arousing. He was every bit the sexy agent, the way his muscles filled out his suits to the way he always seemed so calm and collected. But Jake had a sweet side, too. Paige mused that he genuinely cared for her. She believed him when he said that he wanted to catch who was responsible for the lab. Paige never thought she would be able to trust again. Yet here she was, trusting—needing—someone. It felt good to see the positive side of humanity again. Paige had forgotten it existed in that dismal place.

Her pulse quickened as she leaned forward, her heart thrumming in her chest. Passion roiled within her, a volcano threatening to erupt. Jake's lips were soft against hers. She parted her lips, beckoning him to enter. His firm body pressed against her as his apt tongue massaged hers. He tasted delicious.

Paige ruffled her fingers through his hair as he

hoisted her up on the desk behind her. She wrapped her legs around his body, pressing close against him. The world melted away. Paige forgot all about her missing memories and worries about the loon. All that mattered was Jake.

She reached her fingers up under his blazer, running them along his spine. His muscles flexed against her touch. His mouth pressed harder into hers. Their passion was a fire raging within her. Her animal was hungry for more—needing more.

"Ahem." Someone cleared their throat from across the library, snapping Paige out of her trance. The librarian at the desk, a man with messy brown hair that stuck up like horns, had glowing red cheeks as he shook his head at them.

Paige pulled back from Jake and giggled. "We were...um...studying." She smiled a sheepish grin, knowing how awkward the situation was.

Jake's warm fingers wrapped around her hand, gently tugging her arm. "Sorry, Albert. We were just... leaving," he said, his voice breathless. He led Paige into the corridor, avoiding looking at the other man. After the library door closed behind them, he remarked, "I shouldn't have done that."

Paige raised an eyebrow. Uncertain if she understood him, she asked, "Done what?" She faced him, putting her hands on her hips. *What exactly is he regretting?* she wondered, anger threatening to rise. The heat was beginning to build in her cheeks.

He placed a firm hand on her shoulder, locking his eyes on hers. They were soft and caring, yet something didn't sit right with Paige. His posture was rigid. Jake no longer appeared relaxed around her. She felt like she did something wrong somehow, although she didn't know what. "I should not have kissed you back there." His voice was soft, yet cut her like a knife.

She threw his hand off her shoulder. "I need to get back to my room. Ellie will be worried." Paige felt her hard exterior crumbling. She felt too vulnerable to be out here with *him*. She was stupid to trust him, to open up to him. Now she was regretting the kiss, too. After pivoting on her heel, she turned to go.

"Paige, wait!" Jake called after her. "Let me explain."

Paige's fists balled up tightly as she stopped. Her nails dug into her palms. The world seemed to vanish as she turned to face him, her visage twisted with the intensity of her emotions. "You led me to believe that something else was going on here. And once I decided to trust you, you tell me you regret it!" she spat.

"That's not it at all. I am technically on duty…"

"Oh, I see. Someone saw us, and *you* might get in trouble." Jake's words poured gasoline on the fire within her. He sounded so selfish, and Paige didn't like that at all. It made her wonder if he only *appeared* caring and considerate. *Was the past couple of days just an act on his part? Was this who he truly was?*

"It's not just that. If I saw an agent kissing one of the experiments, I would have a long chat with him about professional behavior, focusing on his job, not taking advantage of the patient…"

"So you're taking advantage of *patients* now?" Paige interrupted. She couldn't believe that he was using language that depersonalized her.

"Maybe." Jake shrugged. "I should be out there tracking down the assholes who did this to you instead of kissing you… in the library of all places. I mean, Albert saw us, and there are strict rules against this sort of thing. I really like you, but maybe we should take it slow while you are being treated here."

Paige didn't know why she was so mad. It seemed disproportionate to what happened, yet she was shaking in rage. She couldn't stop. "I am so sorry that I did not consider how this may have impacted you!" Before Jake could say more, she stormed off down the hall as hot tears poured down her cheeks. Paige could hardly think straight. *Am I nothing more than a broken experiment to him?* Hormones be damned. She wasn't going to be a part of some twisted codependent relationship with a man who wanted to *fix* the broken patient. All she knew was she didn't want to ever see Agent Park again.

11

"Look what was just del..." Ellie, holding up the NAKED box, trailed off as Paige entered the dorm room, slamming the door behind her. "Whoa. What happened?"

Paige shook her head, pacing the room as she willed the image of Jake to fade from memory, hoping it would go away, just like the rest of her life before the lab. "I tried getting down and dirty with Jake. In the library."

"Boom chicka bow wow." Ellie waggled her eyebrows. "Wait, then why do you look so upset?" As if finally seeing the darkness of Paige's mood, Ellie dropped the box and wrung her hands. As she did so, the atmosphere of the room changed. Paige noticed Ellie's shadows even seemed less bubbly, now rolling off of her in large, lazy semi-circles before dissipating.

"We were caught," Paige said, plopping onto her

bed, fearing she would collapse in defeat. "And that's not even the bad part. He said he regretted it."

"Nooo..." Ellie whispered, her eyes widening in confusion. "He didn't!"

"He did. And after I'd worked so hard to be allowed to leave the FUCN'A complex for just *one night,* a single chance to return to normalcy. All that dashed away in an instant."

"It's just a misunderstanding... It's gotta be."

"No, it's more than that. If you knew all of what he said..." She sighed, then shook her head. "No, I'm not going to re-live it all. I'm going to move forward, let his words fade, and get on with things. After all, I'd wanted things to feel normal, and isn't being hurt by someone you trusted one of the most normal things of all?"

Ellie pressed her lips together before saying softly, "I just didn't expect that from Jake."

"Me neither," Paige agreed. "I mean, he appeared so thoughtful and caring. Was it all an act? Tell me, is this something that happens a lot here? The FUC agents making moves on the people they rescued?"

Ellie winced.

"Well?"

"I mean, no, but also yes? I mean, it's not unheard of. The most talked-about couple was Viktor and Renee—that's the famous crocodile FUC agent and his oversized fox—but the way I've heard it told, Viktor did *not* pursue her. She kind of, well, literally, wrapped herself around him and never let go after he liberated her from her lab."

"Fuck." Paige threw her head back on her pillow and stared at the ceiling, not knowing how to feel about the situation. Was this nothing more than countertransference? Was she feeling things for Jake just because he rescued her? The thought nauseated her. It felt more than that to her… but still… "I could really go for a tub of chocolate ice cream right about now." Her mind was twisted in knots. If worrying about the problem wouldn't fix it, junk food would make it feel better, at least.

"How about a Coffee Crisp instead?" Ellie knelt by the NAKED box and pried it open, digging around until she revealed a handful of candy bars. At Paige's puzzled look, Ellie explained, "What? I didn't want to waste what was left on the gift card. While you were on the other computer, searching your name or whatever, I might have thrown in some extra clothes and goodies for the both of us. You don't mind, do you?"

"Of course I don't mind," Paige replied, gratefully taking the candy. "You're the one who got the card in the first place. You deserve some new clothes, too. Heck, I'm sure you'll find someone to have a real date with before I ever get out of this place. I can't believe I was so stupid to think it was all going to be that easy."

"Hey." Ellie crossed the room and sat down next to Paige. "You know what?"

"What?" Paige wiped her tears as she looked at her

friend. She expected Ellie to dismiss her feelings, but she didn't.

"You got out of that lab all on your own. Jake didn't rescue you. You escaped all by yourself. You know that, right?"

"Well, not really. I'm sure if he hadn't shown up, I would have been caught—"

"No!" Ellie cut her off. "Not at all! Don't you dare give him credit for your awesomeness."

"Okay…" Paige said reluctantly. "Hey, can we stop talking about him? Hopefully, he'll go back to his job, and I won't have to see him again, and I think it would help if we never mention Jake Park in this room again."

"Totally. I get it."

"Thanks." It was just one word, but she hoped it carried enough weight to convey to Ellie how much she really appreciated the support.

"Let's not let Agent Par—er, I mean, anything—ruin our day." Ellie moved to the NAKED package and raised an eyebrow. "Who said that you *had* to wear this outfit at the pub? Let's get dolled up just for *us*."

Paige sniffed. Her anger began to dissipate like mist burning off by the morning sun. "Where are we going to go? It's not like they are going to let us leave."

Ellie winked as an impish grin spread across her face, and she began tossing articles of clothing and makeup onto Paige's bed. "Who said anything about leaving? We have an entire campus full of hot cadets at our disposal."

Jake trudged back to the parking lot, his feet heavy feet, his inner fox tail tucked between his legs. A flock of geese in V formation flew overhead, honking as though they laughed at what an idiot Jake had been. The whole thing was disastrous. Jake didn't know if their relationship could recover. Fuck, he wasn't sure there should have even *been* a relationship. Jake didn't want the evil scientist who experimented on Paige out there running around, yet there he was, sucking face with her in the library. But then again, Jake had never felt this way about anyone before. This wasn't just some lustful fling. There were real feelings. He wasn't doing this to balance out what happened to his mom. Jake genuinely wanted to help Paige for her own sake. And there was the way she made him feel. And laugh. Once he got through that prickly exterior, she had a soft underbelly. But when he tried explaining himself, all Jake did was continuously put his foot in his mouth. Why did he always say the wrong things around this woman? She left him so tongue-tied. And what hurt him the most was the further he wedged his foot in his own mouth, the more hurt Paige looked. And angry. Maybe the best thing for her was some space.

If he was that concerned about his job, he should have been more mindful before the kiss. Then he could have prevented it. Since things played out differently, he shouldn't have acted like a callous imbecile. He didn't regret the kiss at all. Had he not been on the job, he wouldn't have cared who walked in on them. The kiss wasn't a mistake, but the timing was. And Jake explained that in the wrong way. Actually, if he would have taken responsibility for his actions and just told Paige he couldn't kiss her again while on duty, the whole situation probably would have been circumvented.

He didn't like knowing that he had hurt Paige. That was the last thing that he wanted to do. Ever. Even without the emotional toll that her recent trauma had taken on her, what Jake said was plain idiotic. But beating himself up about it wasn't going to change anything. It would just make him feel worse.

All the *shoulda, coulda, maybes* haunted Jake as he drove back to the lab to see if there was anything that he'd overlooked. His mistakes with Paige refused to leave his consciousness, making it hard to concentrate, but Jake liked pouring himself into work when upset.

Jake sighed as he stepped into the conference room. He spread the folder of photos of the lab onto the table. Even though Jake and his fellow agents scoured the lab, they weren't looking to link a loon to it. Evidence could have been missed. He couldn't recall anyone ever discussing a random loon at FUCN'A before, so it couldn't be coincidence that an out-of-place loon kept appearing around Paige. Plus, they weren't the type of fowl to sit on your windowsill.

Before leaving WANC, Jake alerted security to a

possible loon shifter on campus, but he intended to figure out what was going on. He promised Paige he would find those responsible. Jake wasn't about to give up over a spat they had. Plus, he was good at his job. He outfoxed bad guys all the time.

He went through the pictures of the dank cells of the lab one at a time, combing every inch of them with a magnifying glass at times. He pushed thoughts of Paige trapped in them from his mind. Knowing she spent a long time in this place was unbearable. He could not even begin to imagine what she must have endured in these walls.

The photographs illustrated a grim scene. Most of the chambers appeared empty, save for a hospital bed and a toilet. Scratches on the walls in some of the rooms must have marked the days the captives spent inside them. It was clear that others were in that lab at some point, but all but Paige were removed by the time of the FUC raid. Then Jake discovered photos of a room that stood out from the others. A bookshelf lined with books sat next to a desk. Notebooks filled the desk. Drawings of birds were scrawled all over the walls. Many of them loons.

Jake remembered seeing this when they first raided the lab. He jumped to the box that held the contents of that cell. He rifled through before picking up a notebook. The writing seemed to be ramblings of a madman. As Jake skimmed through the journals, they slowly began making sense. Some were dated. The ones with older dates were coherent, written as a memoir by someone named Harold, spelling out a story of a man sent to an inpatient psych ward as he battled a psychotic episode. Golden Ridge Psychiatric. Jake remembered hearing that, years ago, it was shut down due to some of the patients going missing. If this was the room of their loon, it appeared he was kidnapped from there, days prior to his planned discharge. From the writings in the notebooks, it appeared the loon had slowly begun losing touch with reality over the past two years. Jake wondered how anyone could hold on to their sanity in that situation. It angered him, knowing that the shifter could have had a happy life—or at least a chance at one—if he hadn't been kidnapped and kept in a cage by evil scientists.

12

"This is way more fun than sulking in our room," Paige declared, sucking down a juice box from the cafeteria. A horde of cadets—many of them shirtless males—ran past them on the track. Paige had hoped the sight of sweat dripping down sculpted naked abs would fully take her mind off Jake, but while it provided a nice distraction, it didn't work. At least not completely.

"See, this place isn't too bad," Ellie remarked, leaning back on the towels they'd borrowed from the shower room. After brainstorming ideas of how to keep Paige's mind off what happened with Jake, they decided their only option was to make the best of their surroundings—mainly by pretending they were lounging on a beach, checking out hot topless men. It only took a little imagination to pretend they were lying on sand instead of the grass near the obstacle course.

A slow smile spread across Paige's face. "We should have made popcorn."

Ellie chuckled. "You know what I am craving?" Dark shadows spiraled off of her hair as she shook it out of her face. In the sunlight, Ellie's shadows were vibrant somehow, seemingly taking on substance.

"What?"

"Maude's Meatless Meatballs." Ellie licked her lips and patted her stomach as if she could taste them. "Too bad it's not Monday."

Paige leaned back on her elbows on the towel. "They're only available on Monday? That's weird. I'm sure you could ask them to whip some up special, don't you think?" Her stomach growled as she said it. All the talk about food made her hungry.

"There's only one way to find out!" Shadows sputtered from Ellie as she jumped to her feet. "You coming?"

Another group of male cadets ran past. "I think I am going to hold our spot while you find us some food."

"Enjoy the view," Ellie squealed before disappearing into her cocoon of bent light.

The sun warmed Paige's skin as she leaned back on the towel, stretching out and closing her eyes. Her body began to relax, even though her mind did not want to. She wished she could banish thoughts of him from her mind, but so far, it had proven impossible. Every sweaty figure that passed her line of sight only reminded her that she wished it was Jake she saw shirtless. And that only reminded her of the shame and embarrassment she felt after he rejected her. It was a deep cut that seemed the open an old wound from her past. An old boyfriend perhaps had done something similar. Paige didn't like the feeling.

The thoughts of Jake flew from her head at the sound of a bird squawking and then landing next to her. She sat up, her body going from almost-relaxed to high alert instantly as the bird ruffled its feathers, leaving a few loose ones in the grass. She swiped out at it, and the bird dodged, taunting her by walking in a circle, bobbing its head with each step before laying a red, unblinking eye on Paige.

"I don't like being stalked, especially by a loon!" she yelled, lunging for the creature.

The waterfowl squabbled and flapped its wings, flying ten more feet away. Paige fumbled to her feet, chasing after the bird. With each attempt to grab it, the bird flitted just out of reach again. "Fine, then just get out of here!" she yelled again.

It stuck a tiny pink tongue out at her.

"Are you mocking me?" She felt crazy asking, but the feathery creature warbled in reply. After giving her a quick wink, it took to the air and floated into the nearby brush with a rustle of leaves.

Paige squinted, searching the brambles for the bird. "You can't hide that easily from me!" she called after the annoying animal as it fluttered out of the brush and into the woods. Paige vaulted into the forest after the thing. It was past time for her to learn the truth about the stalker bird.

The loon laid in wait, nestled into a pile of leaves. It ruffled its feathers, puffing up its tiny body before hiding its head under its wing. Paige tiptoed closer to the bird.

"Are you hiding from me?" she queried, creeping toward the creature. "It's okay, little guy. I just want to talk," she cooed.

"So do we," a voice called out behind her. Before Paige could turn to identify the owner of the voice, the world went dark.

13

Many things were not sitting well with Jake after inspecting the pictures of the cells of the lab. Primarily, why was the loon granted special privileges? His room was the only one with books and writing utensils. Was it a reward for something? Payment? Or was he someone special before he became an experiment? Jake scratched at his chin. Whatever the reason, it was not in any of the writings, nor was there anything left by the scientists to shed light on the situation. All their data was shredded or wiped from the computers. But there was another possibility. If Jake wanted to learn more about this patient, perhaps he could find some answers at Golden Ridge.

From the ramblings in the notebooks, it appeared Harold slowly lost his mind in captivity. Maybe the scientist found him easier to control that way, so they gave him special privileges to coax him into helping him out. It was clear the man was obsessed with loons, but it seemed an unhealthy obsession that went beyond liking the animal that you shifted into. Maybe that was his price for helping the evil scientist out. It didn't make much sense to Jake, but it was clear that poor Harold was driven mad. Maybe he could no longer see the gravity of the situation. Instead, he was hyper-focused on waterfowl. It was difficult to wrap his brain around. Maybe it was a mental escape for Harold.

But first, he wanted to warn Paige that she was probably right about the loon being a shifter. Her safety was his main priority, even if she didn't want to talk to him right now.

Jake was caught off guard when he rounded the corner of the hallway to Paige's dorm room and found swarms of staff and FUC agents pouring from the small room like ants erupting out of an anthill. Their serious manner revealed the fact that something bad happened.

His heart quickened in his chest and a knot formed in his stomach as he pushed through the crowd to enter the room. He'd expected the worst—to see the room ransacked as though there had been an attack—but everything was in place. The only things amiss were the absence of Paige and Ellie sobbing on her bed as she talked to an agent.

"Where's Paige?" Jake asked, afraid of the answer.

Ellie looked up at him with puffy eyes, her bottom lip quivering. "It's all my fault!" she wailed.

"It is not your fault," Jake said firmly. "What happened?"

"Jake! I left her alone outside for maybe twenty minutes, and I came back, and she was gone. I never should have left, but we were on campus, so I thought she'd be safe." Ellie whimpered into the back of her hand.

He listened as Ellie explained, between sniffles, how they took towels and drinks to watch the new cadets work out. The last time she saw Paige was when she left her by the obstacle course and went to WANC for food.

"Sir," one of the agents piped up. "We have agents combing the area where Miss Brennon was last seen. If she is on this campus, we will find her."

But that was the problem. "What if she isn't on campus?"

"I don't think—" the agent started.

"Run down all possibilities," Jake interrupted. "Even her being kidnapped."

Jake's mind reeled. If the loon was after Paige, what did it want? Was this connected to the mystery machine they'd failed to track down? And was there a connection to Golden Ridge Psychiatric?

"I have another lead to track down. Call me if you find anything," Jake ordered the agent. Before leaving, he turned back to Ellie. "I am going to find her."

Jake pulled out his phone to check the location of Golden Ridge. It was a few blocks from the lab, so it jived with the story Paige told about the length of the trip in the van. He called up his team to meet him at the psych ward in case his hunch turned out to be correct. It could be a second lab with more imprisoned shifters. At the very least, he hoped to find Paige and the scientist responsible.

Paige's head pounded. She tried to place a hand on her forehead but couldn't.

She was shackled! She was slumped over on her knees, with her hands bound above her on the two metal piers that flanked her. Paige slowly stood, taking the tension off of her arms.

It was a sensation that she would never forget. The feeling was seared into her memory.

After finally being free, the shackles felt worse than ever. The cold bite of the metal seared her skin as she pulled against the cuffs, even though she knew her struggle was fruitless.

As her eyes focused in the darkness, she recognized her location and what she was shackled to.

The machine room.

The machine.

However, the thick, steel-plated door to the machine chamber had not been shut. She could make out muffled chatter wafting through. She strained her ears, trying to discern what was being said when the voices became louder.

"You promised!" A shrill shout filled the cell. "You said if I brought you the girl, you would make me another loon!"

"You idiot! I can't make any more shifters until *she* opens the portal!" A slap was followed by a whimper.

Fingers curled around the edge of the metal door before footsteps clacked on the concrete floor as a man entered, a sinister smile spread across his familiar face. "Paige is going to be a good girl and scream for me." He ran his fingers through greying hair as his eyes roamed over her body. It was a look Paige remembered from her previous time in the lab.

Paige's wrists stung as she pulled at her bindings. She looked up at the older man defiantly, holding her head high. "I will never scream for you."

He barked a dark laugh. "Harold!"

A new figure shuffled their feet timidly as they entered. Paige caught sight of a man with long, tangled brown hair that swayed in knotted bunches around his gaunt face. "Y-Yes, sir?" He wrung his hands as he neared the older man, brown eyes shifting wildly around the room. When he glanced at Paige, she noted the red handprint on his cheek.

"Do you want to die, Harold?" The scientist spoke with unflinching black eyes, smiling as if talking about the weather. Paige wanted to slap that look right off his face.

"No, D-d-doctor Green," Harold said. The light of the room illuminated his gaunt visage. The man looked starved. His fingers played at the tattered hem of his T-shirt, his eyes trained on the floor as if he were afraid to look at the doctor. "You were to make me a loon friend…and…and let me go." Paige recognized the man's voice from her time at the lab. He was the person she heard whimpering late at night. She was never able to see the others who were held captive with her, but she could hear their voices at night.

"Harold, look at me," Dr. Green said softly and sweetly as he sauntered over to him, placing his hands on his shoulders. Harold reluctantly glanced up before focusing back on the floor. "If you don't make Paige scream, you will get a bullet in your head instead of a friend or freedom."

Harold nodded as if it were a perfectly reasonable statement.

"Do you want that to happen, Paige?" Dr. Green called over his shoulder.

"No," Paige uttered through gritted teeth. She would scream right then if it meant taking out Dr. Green, but she didn't know what would happen if she activated the machine. And even if Harold was the loon who had lured her to her capture, he didn't seem a willing participant in the scheme. He appeared abused and manipulated by the doctor.

"Good." Dr. Green turned to face her, a wide smile spreading slowly across his face making Paige's stomach churn. "Now Paige is going to be a good little girl and help us open this portal to the demon realm. Then, we'll have an array of fun creatures to play with."

Paige couldn't help but roll her eyes. These two were *both* off their rockers!

"And you'll make me a companion?" Harold asked, his voice soft and unsure, like a child afraid to be chastised.

"Of course." The look on Dr. Green's face reminded Paige of a snake. His eyes narrowed, and his lips thinned in another gruesome grin before he turned and slipped out of the room with Harold trailing behind him. "Close the door, you imbecile! Unless you want your brains—"

The door closed with a thud, leaving Paige in silence. The chamber must have been soundproofed. Which made sense. It didn't seem safe for anyone's ears if Paige screamed.

She was seething with anger. The way Dr. Green treated Harold filled her with disgust. But what could she do? Her chains rattled as she tried to free herself in vain. The skin at her wrists reddened as they became raw. Paige was sick of feeling helpless, but she didn't have many options.

"You have to the count of ten to scream, or I will splatter Harold's grey matter over the walls out here." Dr. Green's sinister voice erupted from a speaker in a corner of the room.

The machine behind Paige hummed as Dr. Green brought it to life.

The sound brought memories back to her. *"Ah, precious Paige. We might have failed so many times in the past, but maybe, this time, you'll scream at the right frequency for me. You see, I only have enough electricity to prime the portal. We need the vibrations from your voice to do the rest."*

They *did* something to her that changed her vocal cords. How that could open a portal was beyond Paige's imagination. And to the doctor's dismay, he was never able to engineer her scream to the correct frequency.

But her voice was different the day she escaped the lab. She was certain she could power the portal now. But what would that mean?

"Every other lab is experimenting with humans and shifters, but I'll open a portal to hell and bring back horrible creatures. My creations will be far better than all others, with all-new abilities!"

"One…two…three…" Dr. Green's voice was cold and tinny over the speaker.

Was her refusal to cooperate worth the life of a stranger?

"Four…"

Paige's heart quickened with each number. She chewed her lip, waiting for five. Trying to decide. Weighing her options. *If my scream can rupture eardrums, can it break metal?* She wondered, hoping Dr.

Green had made a grave miscalculation. And for all the failed attempts at opening the portal in the past, her scream probably would do what he intended. Paige leaned forward, getting her mouth as close to the shackles as she could.

The next number never came. "What are you doing?!" Dr. Green's cold voice demanded over the speakers.

The metal dug into her left wrist as she pulled her lips as close as she could to the right shackle. Then she let out a cry that shook the room. Tiny fractures appeared in the metal cuff. It was working.

Just as she broke her arm free, the door to the chamber opened. "Harold, don't!" Dr. Green called after him as he entered the chamber.

His eyes were wide as he pointed a taser at Paige. "You need to do as Dr. Green says." His voice quivered. "I need more loons!" Harold's eyes darted around the room as if looking at other people. "Tell her to do what I want!"

Paige glanced around but saw no one. The machine around her sat quiet. "Harold," she said sweetly. "There's a loon behind me. It must have been created by the machine when I screamed to break my shackle."

"Harold, get out of there!" Dr. Green demanded while keeping his distance. Apparently, hearing Paige's new singing voice in the field was enough for him. It seemed he was trying to keep his distance to minimize future damage to his hearing.

The disheveled man didn't appear to hear Dr. Green. "There's a loon? Behind you?" he asked, creeping forward.

"Yes," Paige coaxed. "I think it's scared." *Just one step closer,* she thought.

Harold tiptoed closer. As soon as Paige saw the distance between them close, she launched a high kick into his jaw. Harold stumbled back.

Paige didn't miss a beat, leaning into her other cuff to scream it open. Out of the corner of her eye, she saw Harold on the ground, covering his ears. She hoped not to permanently injure him. Even though he was a part of the plot to kidnap her, he didn't seem in his right mind.

After ripping free of the last shackle, Paige shifted, ripping through her clothes in the process. She leaped over Harold, who was rocking in a fetal position on the floor. Dr. Green attempted to close the door but was too late. Paige's giant tiger form muscled through the opening, knocking the evil scientist down onto the floor.

Before Paige could pounce, he vanished, swallowed up by his lab coat, which crumpled to the floor. The arm of the garment started swishing around before a tiny field mouse sprang through the opening in the sleeve. The creature attempted to scurry away, but it was no match for a tiger.

Before it could put distance between them, Paige whacked it with her large paw, trapping it.

Before she could decide what to do with the rodent, the door to the room erupted, spilling new bodies inside.

To her relief, she recognized the FUC logo on the jackets and hats.

The good guys had arrived!

As they slowly surrounded her, Paige motioned for them to pay attention to her paw. They seemed to understand what she was trying to say, so she lifted it, exposing the mouse beneath it. An agent scooped it up fast, not allowing Dr. Green time to react and escape. The scientist squirmed, dangling from his tail like a fish on a hook, as the agent placed the shifter in a cage that was brought in.

"Paige!" Her heart jumped at the sound of his voice, and she craned to see him through the crowd.

She couldn't have been happier to finally spot him. He ran to her as she shifted back into her very naked human form. He took off his blazer to wrap around her, his eyes wide with worry as he examined her face. "Are you okay? I was so worried."

She melted into him, breathing a sigh of relief. "Yes, I'm fine. Jake. I-I'm so sorry. I didn't mean to wander off. I…" Her words tumbled out faster than she could think. What she was mad over earlier didn't even matter anymore. It seemed so trivial compared to her kidnapping.

"None of that matters now. I'm just glad you're okay."

A thought occurred to her, and she looked around the room. "What about Harold? The loon? I don't think he's in his right mind."

"He will be looked after. From what I found at the lab, the doctor drove him mad so that he could use him as a pawn to do his dirty work."

It pained Paige to envision. It was true she and other experiments were put through a lot, but Harold was pushed to his limits. Maybe there was no going back for him. *Could he be rehabilitated?* The thought broke loose a buried memory. Paige finally remembered what she used to do for a living.

"I think I know how to piece my life back together," she noted, beaming up at Jake as he put his arm around her. He kept a protective arm around her as he ushered her out of the machine room and down the corridors of the vacant asylum. There was something familiar about the place, which wasn't tied to her being imprisoned in the machine. As they passed the old chart room, Paige saw herself in there—an intern filing paperwork and looking up patient history. "I think I remember something from my previous life," Paige said, squinting as if it could help the memories become clearer back.

"What?"

Paige glanced behind them, down the long corridor. She closed her eyes, trying to focus. "Just down the hall is the nurses' station. Beyond that is the break room where I used to get coffee. I used to come here a few nights after school as part of their interning program."

"You can tell me all about it over dinner." Jake squeezed her shoulder as they stepped out into the dying light of the day.

14

Paige couldn't believe her counselor let her leave campus for dinner with Jake after the ordeal with the kidnapping and the machine, but Jake convinced Dr. Daya that Paige had more than earned it.

Over dinner at the Hub—a fun little pub in town that was more crowded than she would have expected from a town that size—Paige pieced together bits of her lost memories like a jigsaw puzzle. Not all of it came back, but from what she gathered, she used to be a therapist of some sort. The strongest memories were from her internship at Golden Ridge. She told him about everything she could recall of her father, and he promised to help her find him.

After she muddled through her thoughts, it was Jake's turn. She listened intently as he explained to her why he took his job so personally. Her heart broke as he recounted the ordeal his mother had gone through.

"I just never want anyone else to have to live like that, looking over their shoulder for the rest of their lives."

"I can understand that," Paige said, knowing that the way he reacted after the library was because he cared deeply for her. It wasn't because she was broken or because he had some kind of savior complex.

"So, we're okay?"

She nodded and turned a smile on him. "Very okay. In fact, I'm wondering if we could go to your place for some dessert?"

"Are you sure you're ready?" Jake asked.

Paige thought long and hard about if she wanted to be with Jake for the right reasons. What she liked most about Jake was she felt more stable with him. He was able to bring her back to center when she felt out of control. And he took everything she said seriously, even when she was afraid of the loon. Paige knew she'd be fine without him, yet enjoyed spending time with him. And she didn't want him to help fix her. It had all the elements of a healthy relationship. "I am," she said after careful deliberation.

She followed Jake to his vehicle, smiling all the way. Even though she went through a traumatic ordeal, it felt like her life had found its own way to put itself back together. "You know, I've been thinking," Paige started as she sat down and put on her seatbelt.

"What?" Jake asked, his dark eyes warm and inviting. Paige loved how he was so easy to talk to.

"After I get cleared by my counselor, I want to start the training program as a cadet at FUCN'A to counsel other rescued shifters as they are rehabilitated. I feel like I ended up here for a reason. Everyone here has been so supportive of me, and I want to be able to do that for others. That's what brought me to counseling in the first place."

Jake smiled. "I think that sounds great."

After a short drive, they pulled into the driveway of Jake's house. It was a few minutes drive from the main strip of the town and WANC. It was a charming Tudor-style home with a sweeping roof over the entrance. Large, flat stones were linked together, forming the wide chimney in the front, giving the house a cottage feel.

"It's so beautiful." Paige tried to imagine how the front gardens would look at the height of summer.

"Thank you," Jake said as he parked his SUV. "I wanted a home that was relaxing so I can take a break from work here and forget the rest of the world exists."

Paige turned to him. "Does that work?"

Jake smiled, his eyes dancing. "Not always."

Paige chuckled as she got out, following Jake down the brick walkway and then through the entranceway. The interior was filled with potted plants and warm colors on the walls. She found it incredibly relaxing. Everything was just perfect, including Jake. He didn't always say the right things, but his heart was in a good place. He would do anything for her. Paige appreciated that he would even give her space if needed.

"Do you want me to put on some coffee?" Jake asked after giving her a brief tour, ending in the bedroom. "What?" Jake inquired after Paige didn't reply. His eyes roamed over her body.

She felt like her old self again. At least what she could remember of her old self. Paige started to realize that it didn't matter if her memories didn't all return. She could focus on building her life going forward. And Jake was a big part of that.

"I was just thinking about you." A wide smile spread across her face as the passion ignited within her.

Paige hooked her fingers into Jake's belt loop and pulled him forward. Their body heat mingled as he pressed against her, pressing his soft lips into hers. She parted her lips, wanting a deeper kiss. His tongue entered her mouth and flitted about, massaging hers as he trailed his fingers up her spine. Just the taste of him was enough to ignite her appetite. His touch was tender, delicate. It lit a fire within her. Her heart beat rapidly, spreading heat through her limbs. A tingling spread from her loins. Her passion was a volcano, and it was erupting.

His roaming hands found their way to her waist, slowly easing her out of her pants. They fell to the floor in a pile at her feet. Jake eased her onto the bed, weaving a stream of kisses up her torso. Each one was like electricity, leaving an array of goosebumps in their wake. Her core heated up with each lingering touch. She wanted— no, needed —Jake now. He ignited a passion in her soul that Paige didn't know existed. He also helped her to find her balance when angry at the world. Plus, he was one sexy fox. That was always a plus.

Even though she didn't have access to all her memories, she knew that she had never felt this way about anyone else. Paige knew that Jake was the first man she had ever been comfortable around outside of her family. The only man she had ever trusted this deeply. There was a strong connection between them that she had never had before. But he was more than that. Jake was her guiding light out of the darkness. He was her beacon of hope that some people were trying to make the world a better place.

Paige freed Jake from his pants, his manhood springing free. She needed to feel him inside her. It was closeness that she yearned for. She thrummed with desire. She guided him to her wet sex. Jake glided inside of her, causing a moan to escape her lips. He kissed the corner of her mouth before entering her fully. It was a brief tease, making her want him even more. Paige pulled him closer, pressing her hands on his lower back. His scent was intoxicating. Paige couldn't get enough of him. She wanted to be in this moment forever.

The world melted away. It was just Jake and her, together, becoming one. She glided her fingers across his warm back as he found a rhythm that made her insides tense around him. Her muscles pulsed around him. Her flesh tingled with the electricity of passion. Paige felt like she would burst from the intensity of the pleasure. Her senses were overwhelmed. She wanted to scream but was afraid to shatter the windows—and Jake. Instead, she bit his shoulder as he climaxed within her. Her sex pulsed with pleasure as she burst around his cock in ecstasy. She held Jake close, not wanting the moment to end.

Jake lay next to Paige on the bed. He slowly stroked her stomach, propped up on his elbow, taking her in. She was so beautiful, and she wanted to be with him. He couldn't believe it. She was smart, funny, caring, and a badass when she needed to be. He was her rock, and she, his inspiration. He couldn't wait until they started building a life together as Paige started her career as a counselor at WANC.

He hoped that he would be able to hold up his end of his promise. Jake wanted more than anything to track down the rest of the scientists from the lab to put her worries to rest and end her nightmare. While it was great that they'd apprehended Harold and Dr.

Green, Jake felt that there were more out there, especially other shifters who they weren't able to rescue. At least Harold would finally get the help he deserved, and Dr. Green was being held accountable for the atrocities he committed. But that was all for another day. For right now, he wanted to enjoy his time with Paige.

"What?" Paige asked breathlessly, her green eyes roaming over his naked body. He loved the way she looked at him. There was always a hunger in her eyes.

"I was just thinking about how much you mean to me." A grin spread across his face. She brought him peace and happiness. Jake couldn't believe someone could feel this content.

The moment was so perfect. Jake wanted it to never end.

The light of the computer monitor basked the laboratory in a blue glow, illuminating the flash drive in his hand. If Dr. Smith had been there for Dr. Green's ridiculous portal experiment, he'd be up shit's creek with the other two.

Instead, he was free and forming a revised plan as he waded in the silence of his new lab space.

Harold's usefulness may have run out, but before he went off with Dr. Green to get kidnapped by FUC agents, he hadn't shut up about all he'd seen on the

FUCN'A campus—including the interesting shifter who could bend light in strange ways.

Dr. Smith assumed it was just the usual ramblings from delusional Harold but decided to get more information just in case. And it paid off. Dr. Smith's newest minion had managed to gain access into WANC and download the files on the shadow girl. Now Dr. Smith held the cat's secrets in the unassuming device in his hot little hand.

After pushing the flash drive into the computer, Dr. Smith smiled wickedly at the new information he had obtained.

Maybe his years of experimenting weren't a waste of time after all. He had just identified the tool he needed to complete his research. Now he just needed to capture her and put her to use. And if she refused, Dr. Smith would figure out how to force the girl to submit to his demands. After all, Dr. Smith knew how to persuade people. Everyone had their price. This girl would be no different.

Ellie Talbot was in his crosshairs. And Dr. Smith intended to test all her wonderful abilities.

The End

Or is it? Stay tuned for Dr. Smith's plan, coming in Shadow Cat and the Sloth by Scarlet Fox (releasing summer 2022)!

And there are more FUC Academy books from other authors coming your way!

To find out more about these books and more, visit worlds.EveLanglais.com or sign up for the EveL Worlds newsletter. If you haven't already downloaded the **free Academy intro** (written by Eve Langlais) make sure you grab it at worlds.evelanglais.com/wordpress/book/fucacademy1!

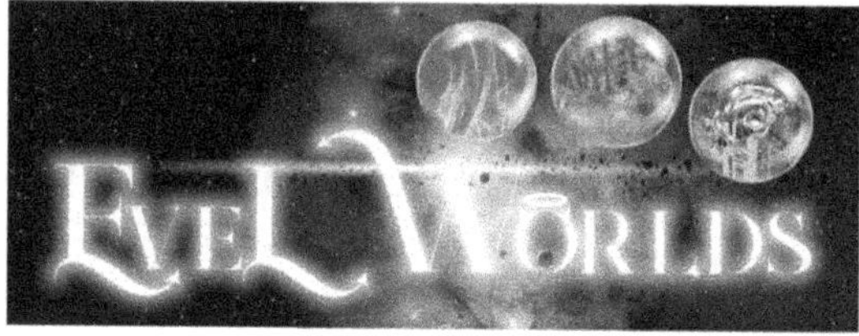

ABOUT THE AUTHOR

Scarlet Fox (aka B.L. Carroll) enjoys writing when she isn't at her day job. Creating romances that push at gender norms is a fun challenge for her. Scarlet's alter ego loves writing mysteries and supernatural thrillers with a strong female lead.

Destigmatizing mental health and other internal struggles are recurring themes in her fiction. Other hobbies include painting, singing, or going for walks. Coffee is a necessity, as is reading. She lives in western New York with her fur babies and partner.

Website: scarletfoxauthor.wixsite.com

Newsletter sign-up: subscribepage.com/scarlet-fox

facebook.com/ScarletFoxAuthor

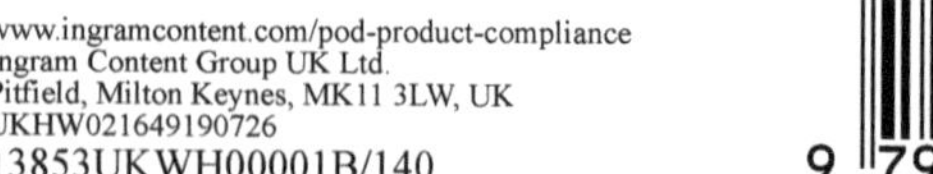
www.ingramcontent.com/pod-product-compliance
Ingram Content Group UK Ltd.
Pitfield, Milton Keynes, MK11 3LW, UK
UKHW021649190726
13853UKWH00001B/140

9 798201 145514